FLUSH

www.kidsatrandomhouse.co.uk

Also by Carl Hiaasen:

Hoot

CARL HIAASEN

FLUSH

Doubleday

LONDON · NEW YORK · TORONTO · SYDNEY · AUCKLAND

This is a work of fiction. All names and characters are either invented or used fictitiously. The legend of the green flash, however, is well known in the Florida Keys.

FLUSH
A DOUBLEDAY BOOK 0 385 60953 1 (hb)
0 385 60954 X (tpb)

First published in the USA by Alfred A. Knopf,
an imprint of Random House Children's Books,
and simultaneously in Canada by Random House of Canada Ltd
Published in Great Britain by Doubleday,
an imprint of Random House Children's Books

Knopf edition published 2005
This edition published 2005

1 3 5 7 9 10 8 6 4 2

Papers used by Random House Children's Books are natural, recyclable products made from wood grown in sustainable forests. The manufacturing processes conform to the environmental regulations of the country of origin.

Set in Sabon by Palimpsest Book Production Limited,
Polmont, Stirlingshire

RANDOM HOUSE CHILDREN'S BOOKS
61-63 Uxbridge Road, London W5 5SA
A division of The Random House Group Ltd

RANDOM HOUSE AUSTRALIA (PTY) LTD
20 Alfred Street, Milsons Point, Sydney,
New South Wales 2061, Australia

RANDOM HOUSE NEW ZEALAND LTD
18 Poland Road, Glenfield, Auckland 10, New Zealand

RANDOM HOUSE (PTY) LTD
Endulini, 5A Jubilee Road, Parktown 2193, South Africa

THE RANDOM HOUSE GROUP Limited Reg. No. 954009
www.kidsatrandomhouse.co.uk

A CIP catalogue record for this book is available from the British Library.

Printed and bound in Great Britain
by Mackays of Chatham plc, Chatham, Kent

For the mighty Quinn

ONE

The deputy told me to empty my pockets: two quarters, a penny, a stick of bubble gum, and a roll of grip tape for my skateboard. It was pitiful.

'Go on inside. He's waiting for you,' the deputy said.

My dad was sitting alone at a bare metal table. He looked pretty good, all things considered. He wasn't even handcuffed.

'Happy Father's Day,' I said.

He stood up and gave me a hug. 'Thanks, Noah,' he said.

In the room there was another deputy – a broad, jowly bear standing next to the door that led to the jail cells. I guess his job was to make sure I wasn't smuggling a hacksaw to my father so that he could break out.

'It's good they let you keep your own clothes,' I said to Dad. 'I figured they'd make you put on one of those dorky uniforms.'

'I'm sure they will, sooner or later.' He shrugged. 'You doing OK?'

'How come you won't let Mom bail you out?' I asked.

'Because it's important for me to be here right now.'

'Important how? She says you'll lose your job if you stay locked up.'

'She's probably right,' my dad admitted.

He'd been driving a taxi for the past year and a half. Before that he was a fishing guide – a good one, too, until the coast guard took away his captain's licence.

He said, 'Noah, it's not like I robbed a bank or something.'

'I know, Dad.'

'Did you go see what I did?'

'Not yet,' I said.

He gave me a wink. 'It's impressive.'

'Yeah, I bet.'

He was in a surprisingly good mood. I'd never been to a jail before, though honestly it wasn't much of a jail. Two holding cells, my dad told me. The main county lockup was miles away in Key West.

'Mom wants to know if she should call the lawyer,' I said.

'I suppose.'

'The same one from last time? She wasn't sure.'

'Yeah, he's all right,' my father said.

His clothes were rumpled and he looked tired, but

he said the food was decent and the police were treating him fine.

'Dad, what if you just said you're sorry and offered to pay for what you did?'

'But I'm *not* sorry for what I did, Noah. The only thing I'm sorry about is that you've got to see me locked up like an axe murderer.'

The other times my dad had gotten in trouble, they wouldn't let me come to the jail because I was too young.

'I'm not a common criminal.' Dad reached across and put a hand on my arm. 'I know right from wrong. Good from bad. Sometimes I just get carried away.'

'Nobody thinks you're a criminal.'

'Dusty Muleman sure does.'

'That's because you sunk his boat,' I pointed out. 'If you just paid to get it fixed, maybe then—'

'That's a seventy-three-footer,' my dad cut in. 'You've got to know what you're doing to sink one of those pigs. You ought to go have a look.'

'Maybe later,' I said.

The deputy standing by the door made a grunting noise and held up five chubby fingers, which was the number of minutes left before he took my father back to the cell.

'Is your mom still ticked off at me?' Dad asked.

'What do you think?'

'I tried to explain it to her, but she wouldn't listen.'

'Then maybe you can explain it to me,' I said. 'I'm old enough to understand.'

Dad smiled. 'I believe you are, Noah.'

My father was born and raised here in Florida, so he grew up on the water. His dad – my Grandpa Bobby – ran a charter boat out of Haulover Marina on Miami Beach. Grandpa Bobby passed away when I was little, so I honestly didn't remember him. We'd heard different stories about what happened – one was that his appendix burst; another was that he got hurt real bad in a bar fight. All we knew for sure is that he took his fishing boat down to South America on some sort of job, and he never came back.

One day a man from the US State Department showed up at our house and told my parents that Grandpa Bobby was dead and buried near some little village in Colombia. For some weird reason they couldn't bring his body home for a funeral – I knew this because I'd seen the paperwork. My dad kept a file, and at least four or five times a year he would write to Washington, DC, asking someone to please help get his father's coffin back to Florida. This is, like, ten years later. Mom worked with my dad on the letters – she's a legal secretary, and she gets straight to the point.

My mom and dad first met while they were standing in line to pay speeding tickets at the Dade County Courthouse, and they got married six weeks later. I know this for a fact because Mom put the speeding tickets in a scrapbook, along with their wedding pictures and stuff like that. The ticket my mother got was for driving forty-four miles an hour in a thirty-five-mile-per-hour zone. My father's ticket was much worse – he was doing ninety-three on the turnpike. In the album Dad's ticket looks sort of lumpy and wrinkled because he'd crumpled it into a ball when the state trooper handed it to him. My mother said she used a laundry iron to flatten it out before pasting it next to hers in the scrapbook.

About a year after they got married, my parents moved down to the Keys. I'm sure this was Dad's idea, because he'd been coming here ever since he was a kid and he hated the big city. I was actually born in a 1989 Chevrolet Caprice on US Highway One, my dad racing up the eighteen-mile stretch from Key Largo to the mainland. He was trying to get my mother to the hospital in Homestead. She was lying in the back seat of the car, and that's where I was born. Mom did it all by herself – she didn't tell my dad to pull over and stop because she didn't want him interfering. They still argue about this. (She says he's got a tendency to get overexcited, which is the understatement of the century.) He didn't even realize I was born until they got to Florida City and I started bawling.

Abbey came along three years later. Dad talked my mom into naming her after one of his favourite writers, some weird old bird who's buried out West in the middle of a desert.

Most of my friends aren't crazy about their sisters, but Abbey's all right. Maybe it's not cool to say so, but the truth is the truth. She's funny and tough and not nearly as irritating as most of the girls at school. Over the years Abbey and I developed a pretty good system: she keeps an eye on Mom, and I keep an eye on Dad. Sometimes, though, I need extra help.

'So, what's the deal?' Abbey asked after I got back from the jail.

We were sitting at the kitchen table. For lunch Mom had fixed us the usual, ham-and-cheese sand-wiches.

'He says he got carried away again,' I said.

Abbey raised her eyebrows and snorted. 'No duh.'

Mom set two glasses of milk on the table. 'Noah, why does he insist on staying in jail? It's Father's Day, for heaven's sake.'

'I guess he's trying to make a point.'

'All he's making,' my sister said, 'is a jackass of himself.'

'Hush, Abbey,' Mom told her.

'He said it's OK to call the lawyer,' I added.

'He's not pleading guilty?' Abbey asked. 'How can he *not* plead guilty? He did it, didn't he?'

'It's still smart to have an attorney,' said my mother. She seemed much calmer now. When the police first called, she'd gotten real mad and said some pretty harsh things about Dad. Honestly, I couldn't blame her. Even for him this was a major screw-up.

'Noah, how are you doing?' she asked.

I knew she was worried that the jailhouse visit had shaken me up, so I told her I was fine.

She said, 'I'm sure it wasn't easy seeing your father behind bars.'

'They brought him to a private room,' I said. 'He wasn't even wearing handcuffs.'

My mother frowned slightly. 'Still, it's not a happy picture.'

Abbey said, 'Maybe he ought to plead insanity.'

Mom ignored her. 'Your father has many good qualities,' she said to me, 'but he's not the most stable role model for a young man like yourself. He'd be the first to admit it, Noah.'

Whenever I get this speech, I listen patiently and don't say a word. She won't come right out and say so, but Mom worries that I'm too much like my dad.

'Drink your milk,' she said, and went to the den to call our lawyer, a man named Mr Shine.

As soon as we were alone, Abbey reached over and twisted the hair on my arm. 'Tell me everything,' she said.

'Not now.' I jerked my head toward the doorway. 'Not with Mom around.'

Abbey said, 'It's all right. She's on the phone.'

I shook my head firmly and took a bite of my sandwich.

'Noah, are you holding out on me?' my sister asked.

'Finish your lunch,' I said, 'then we'll go for a ride.'

The *Coral Queen* had gone down stern first in twelve feet of water. Her hull had settled on the marly bottom at a slight angle with the bow aiming upward.

She was a big one, too. Even at high tide the top two decks were above the water line. It was like a big ugly apartment building had fallen out of the sky and landed in the basin.

Abbey hopped off my handlebars and walked to the water's edge. She planted her hands on her hips and stared at the crime scene.

'Whoa,' she said. 'He really did it this time.'

'It's bad,' I agreed.

The *Coral Queen* was one of those gambling boats where passengers line up to play blackjack and electronic poker, and to stuff their faces at the all-you-can-eat buffet. It didn't sound like a ton of fun to me, but the *Coral Queen* was packed to the rafters every night.

There was one major difference between Dusty Muleman's operation and the gambling cruises up in Miami: the *Coral Queen* didn't actually go anywhere. That's one reason it was so popular.

By Florida law, gambling boats are supposed to travel at least three miles offshore – beyond the state boundaries – before anyone is allowed to start betting. Rough weather is real bad for business because lots of customers get seasick. As soon as they start throwing up, they quit spending money.

According to my father, Dusty Muleman's dream was to open a gambling boat that never left the calm and safety of its harbour. That way the passengers would never get too queasy to party.

Only Indian tribes are allowed to run casino operations in Florida, so Dusty somehow persuaded a couple of rich Miccosukees from Miami to buy the marina and make it part of their reservation. Dad said the government raised a stink but later backed off because the Indians had better lawyers.

Anyway, Dusty got his gambling boat – and he got rich.

My dad had waited until three in the morning, when the last of the crew had gone, to sneak aboard. He'd untied the ropes and started one of the engines and idled out to the mouth of the basin, where he'd opened the seacocks and cut the hoses and disconnected the bilge pumps and then dived overboard.

The *Coral Queen* had gone down crosswise in the channel, which meant that no other vessels could get in or out of the basin. In other words, Dusty Muleman wasn't the only captain in town who wanted to strangle my dad on Father's Day.

I locked my bike to a buttonwood tree and walked down to the charter docks, Abbey trailing behind. Two small skiffs and a coast guard inflatable were nosing around the *Coral Queen*. We could hear the men in the skiffs talking about what had to be done to float the boat. It was a major project.

'He's lost his marbles,' Abbey muttered.

'Who – Dad? No way,' I said.

'Then why did he do it?'

'Because Dusty Muleman has been dumping his holding tank into the water,' I said.

Abbey grimaced. 'Yuck. From the toilets?'

'Yep. In the middle of the night, when there's nobody around.'

'That is so gross.'

'And totally illegal,' I said. 'He only does it to save money.'

According to my father, Dusty Muleman was such a pathetic cheapskate that he wouldn't pay to have the *Coral Queen*'s sewage hauled away. Instead his crew had standing orders to flush the waste into the basin, which was already murky. The tide later carried most of the filth out to open water.

'But why didn't Dad just call the coast guard?' my sister asked. 'Wouldn't that have been the grown-up thing to do?'

'He told me he tried. He said he called everybody he could think of, but they could never catch Dusty in the act,' I said. 'Dad thinks somebody's tipping him off.'

'Oh, please,' Abbey groaned.

Now she was starting to annoy me.

'When the wind and the current are right, the poop from the gambling boat floats out of the basin and down the shoreline,' I said, 'straight to Thunder Beach.'

Abbey made a pukey face. 'Ugh. So that's why they close the park sometimes.'

'You know how many kids go swimming there? What Dusty's doing can make you real sick at both ends. Hospital-sick, Dad says. So it's not only disgusting, it's dangerous.'

'Yeah, but—'

'I didn't say it was right, Abbey, what Dad did. I'm only telling you why.'

My father hadn't even tried to get away. After swimming back to the dock, he'd sat down in a folding chair, opened a can of root beer, and watched the

Coral Queen go down. He was still there at dawn, sleeping, when the police arrived.

'So what now?' Abbey asked.

A dark bluish slick surrounded the boat, and the men in the coast guard inflatable were laying out yellow floating bumpers, to keep the oil and grease from spreading. By sinking the *Coral Queen*, my father himself had managed to make quite a mess.

I said, 'Dad asked me to help him.'

Abbey made a face. 'Help him what – break out of jail?'

'Get serious.'

'Then what, Noah? Tell me.'

I knew she wasn't going to like it. 'He wants me to help him nail Dusty Muleman,' I said.

A long silence followed, so I figured Abbey was thinking up something snarky to say. But it turned out that she wasn't.

'I didn't give Dad an answer yet,' I said.

'I already know your answer,' said my sister.

'His heart's in the right place, Abbey. It really is.'

'It's not his heart I'm worried about, it's his brain,' she said. 'You'd better be careful, Noah.'

'Are you going to tell Mom?'

'I haven't decided.' She gave me a sideways look that told me she probably wouldn't.

Like I said, my sister's all right.

TWO

Lucky for us, it was summertime and school was out. That meant that Abbey and I didn't have to face all the other kids at once. It's a pretty small town and news gets around fast, so by now it was no secret that our father was in the slammer for sinking Dusty Muleman's casino boat. Everybody would be talking about it.

The kid I most didn't want to see was Jasper Muleman Jr, who was Dusty's son. He was a well-known jerk, which I partly blamed on the fact that his parents had named him Jasper. That would be enough to make anybody mean and mad at the world.

Unfortunately, he was at the marina the next morning when I stopped by to see the salvage crew float the *Coral Queen*. Scuba divers were feeding fat black hoses into the sunken half of the boat, though I couldn't tell if they were pumping water out or pumping air in. I spotted Jasper Jr before he spotted me, but for some reason I didn't sneak away. I just stood around watching the divers wrestle with the hoses until Jasper Jr came over and called me a name that wasn't very original.

'I'm sorry about what happened to your dad's boat,' I said, trying my hardest to sound sincere.

When Jasper Jr shoved me, I wasn't totally surprised. He isn't a big kid but he's wiry and strong, and he likes to fight. It's one of the only things he does well.

'Lay off,' I said, and naturally he pushed me again.

'Your crazy father sunk our boat!' Jasper Jr snarled.

'I said I was sorry.'

'You're gonna pay for this, Underwood.'

Normally I try to stick to the truth, but I wasn't in the mood to get punched in the face, which is what Jasper Jr had in mind. So, to calm him down, I said, 'I just came by to see if I could help.'

'I'm so sure.'

'Honest!'

Jasper Jr sneered, which is another thing he's good at. I found myself studying the shape of his head, which reminded me of an extra-large walnut. He wore his hair in a buzz cut, and you could see shiny lumps and crinkles in the skin of his scalp. Maybe everybody's skull is knobby and weird underneath their hair, but on Jasper Jr it made him look even meaner.

He said, 'Underwood, I'm gonna kick your butt from here to Miami.'

'I don't think so.'

'Yeah? And why don't you think so, dorkface?'

'Because your dad's about to come over here and kick yours,' I said, which was true.

Dusty Muleman had been hollering for his son from the other side of the basin. Jasper Jr hadn't heard him because he was too busy messing with me, and now his father was seriously ticked off. I pointed across the water to where Dusty Muleman stood glaring, his arms folded. Jasper Jr spun around and saw for himself.

'Uh-oh,' he said, and took off running to join his father. 'I'll get you later!' he hollered at me over one shoulder.

A few minutes later Abbey showed up, and we hung around until the *Coral Queen* was off the bottom. We were surprised to see how easily they got her up, but of course there weren't any holes in the hull or other damage that needed patching. My father had just pulled the plugs, basically.

'How does Dad know it's the casino boat doing the dumping?' Abbey asked.

'Because they never had to close Thunder Beach before the *Coral Queen* got here. They never had a problem with poop in the water until now,' I said.

A small crowd had gathered to see the operation, but Abbey and I stayed off by ourselves, on the far side of the basin. We didn't want to make Dusty Muleman any madder than he already was.

'What a phoney,' my sister said. 'Just look at him.'

At one time Dusty Muleman had been an ordinary fishing guide, the same as my father. Their skiffs were berthed next to each other at a place called Ted's Marina. In the summertime, when business slowed down, Dusty would head out to Colorado and work at a dude ranch, taking tourists into the mountains for brook trout. Then one September he came back to the Keys and put his skiff up for sale. He told Dad and the other guides that he'd inherited some money from a rich uncle who'd died in an elephant stampede in Africa. I remember Mom's eyes narrowing when Dad told us the story – it was the same look I get whenever I tell her I'm done with my homework and she knows better.

As for my father, he said anything was possible, even Dusty Muleman being related to a dead millionaire. Not long after he quit guiding, Dusty bought the *Coral Queen*, got her outfitted for gambling, and partnered up with the Miccosukees. That wasn't even two years ago, and now he was one of the richest men in Monroe County, or so he said. He drove up and down Highway One in a black Cadillac SUV, and he wore bright flowered shirts and smoked real Cuban cigars, just to let the world know what a big shot he was. But according to Dad, Dusty still showed up every night at the casino boat, to count the money personally.

Abbey said, 'Muleman'll have that tub fixed up good as new in a week. What was Dad thinking? If he was serious, he would've burned the darn thing to the water line.'

'Don't give him any ideas,' I said.

Lice Peeking lived in a trailer park on the old road that runs parallel to the main highway. I got there at lunchtime but he was still asleep. When I offered to come back later, his girlfriend said no, she'd be happy to wake him. She was a large lady with bright blonde hair and a barbed-wire tattoo around one of her biceps. My dad had told me about her. He'd said to make sure I was extra polite.

The girlfriend disappeared down the hallway and came back half a minute later, leading Lice Peeking by his belt. He didn't look so good and he smelled even worse – a combination of beer and B.O. was my guess.

'Who're you?' he demanded, then sagged down on an old sofa.

The girlfriend said, 'I'm off to the store.'

'Don't forget my cigarettes,' Lice Peeking told her.

'No way. You promised to quit.'

'Aw, gimme a break, Shelly.'

They argued for a while and seemed to forget they had company. I pretended to look at the aquarium, which had pea-green slime on the glass and exactly one live fish swimming in the water.

Finally, Lice Peeking's girlfriend said he was hopeless and snatched the wallet out of his jeans and stomped out the door. When he got himself together, he asked once more who I was.

'Noah Underwood,' I said.

'Paine's boy?'

'That's right. He asked me to come see you.'

'About what?'

'Mr Muleman,' I said.

From Lice Peeking's throat came a sound that was either a chuckle or a cough. He fished under one of the sofa cushions until he found a half-smoked, mushed-up cigarette, which he balanced in a crusty corner of his mouth.

'I don't s'pose you got a match,' he said.

'No, sir.'

He dragged himself to the kitchenette and knocked around until he came up with a lighter. He fired up the mouldy butt and sucked on it for a solid minute without even glancing in my direction. The smoke was making me sick to my stomach, but I couldn't leave until I got an answer. For two years, until last

Christmas Eve, Lice Peeking had worked as a mate on Dusty Muleman's casino boat.

'Mr Peeking?' I said. His real name was Charles, but Dad said everyone had called him Lice, for obvious reasons, since elementary school. It didn't look like his bathing habits had improved much since then.

'What do you want, boy?' he snapped.

'It's about the *Coral Queen*. My dad says Mr Muleman is dumping the holding tank into the marina basin.'

Lice Peeking propped himself against the wall of the trailer. 'Really? Well, let's just say that's true. What's it got to do with you or me or the price of potatoes?'

'My father's in jail,' I said, 'for sinking that boat.'

'Aw, go on.'

'I'm serious. I thought everybody'd heard by now.'

Lice Peeking started laughing so hard, I thought he might have an asthma attack and fall on the floor. Obviously the news about my father had brightened his day.

'Please,' I said, 'will you help us?'

He stopped laughing and snuffed the nub of his cigarette on the countertop. 'Now why would I do a dumb fool thing like that? Help you do *what*?'

I explained how the toilet scum from the gambling boat flowed down the shoreline to Thunder Beach.

'Where the turtles lay their eggs,' I said, 'and all the kids go swimming.'

Lice Peeking shrugged. 'Say I was to help you – what's in it for me?'

Dad had warned me that Lice Peeking wasn't accustomed to doing something simply because it was decent and right. He'd predicted that Lice Peeking might demand something in return.

'We don't have much,' I said.

'Aw, that's too bad.' He made like he was playing a violin.

I knew money would be tight at our house as long as Dad was in jail – my mother only works part-time at the law firm, so the pay isn't so hot.

'What about my dad's truck?' I asked. 'It's a ninety-seven Dodge pickup.' Giving it up was my father's idea.

'No, I already got wheels,' Lice Peeking said. 'Anyway, I'm not s'posed to drive on account of they yanked my licence. What else?'

I thought of offering him Dad's fishing skiff, but I couldn't bring myself to do it. It was a cool little boat.

'Let me talk to my father,' I said.

'You do that.'

'Will you at least promise to think about it?'

'You listen here,' Lice Peeking said. 'What do I care about baby sea turtles? I got my own daily survival to worry about.'

He pointed to the door and followed me out. I was halfway down the steps of the trailer before I got up the nerve to ask one more question.

'How come you don't work for Mr Muleman any more?'

'Because he fired me,' Lice Peeking said. 'Didn't your old man tell you?'

'No, sir, he didn't.'

To keep from wobbling, Lice Peeking braced himself with both arms in the doorway. His face was pasty in the sunlight, and his eyes were glassy and dim. He looked like a sick old iguana, yet according to my dad, he was only twenty-nine. It was hard to believe.

'Ain't you gonna ask why I got canned?' he said. 'It was for stealin'.'

'Did you do it?'

'Yep, I sure did.'

'How much?' I asked.

Lice Peeking grinned. 'It wasn't money I stole from Dusty,' he said. 'It was Shelly.'

'Oh.'

'What can I say? I needed a lady with a big heart and a valid driver's licence.'

I said, 'I'll be back after I see my father.'

'Whatever,' said Lice Peeking. 'I'm gonna hunt down a beer.'

*

My mother says that being married to my father is like having another child to watch after, one who's too big and unpredictable to put in time-out. Sometimes, when Mom and Dad are arguing, she threatens to pack up our stuff and take me and Abbey out of the Keys to 'go start a normal life'. I think my mother loves my dad but she just can't understand him. Abbey says Mom understands him perfectly fine, but she just can't figure out how to fix him.

When I got back from the trailer park, my mother was in the kitchen chopping up onions. That's how I knew she'd been crying. Nobody in our family likes onions, and the only time Mom ever fixes them is when she's upset. That way she can tell Abbey and me that it's only the onions making her eyes water.

I knew she'd been to the jail, so I asked, 'How's Dad?'

My mother didn't look up. 'Oh, he's just dandy,' she said.

'Is there any news?'

'What do you mean, Noah?'

'About when he's getting out.'

'Well, that's entirely up to him,' Mom said. 'I've offered to put up his bail, but apparently he'd rather sit alone in a cramped, roach-infested cell than be home with his family. Maybe the lawyer can talk some sense into him.'

Of course I couldn't tell her what my father had asked me to do. She would've raced back to the jail, reached through the bars and throttled him.

'Think they'll let me visit him again?' I asked.

'I don't see why not. It isn't as if his social schedule is all booked up.'

From the tone of her voice I knew she was highly irritated with my father.

'I spoke to your Aunt Sandy and your Uncle Del,' she said. 'They offered to call him in jail and try to talk some sense into him, but I told them not to bother.'

Aunt Sandy and Uncle Del are Dad's older sister and brother. They live in Miami Beach – Sandy in a high-rise condominium with a gym on the top floor, and Del in a nice house with a tennis court in the backyard. This is a sensitive subject at our home.

Several years after my grandfather disappeared in South America, a large amount of money was discovered in a safe-deposit box that he'd kept at a bank up in Hallandale. Nobody ever told Abbey or me exactly how much was there, but it must have been a lot. I remember Dad talking about it with my mother, who always wondered how a charter-boat captain could afford to put away so much cash. She had a point, too – nobody we knew ever got rich in the fishing business.

Anyway, Grandpa Bobby had left instructions that

the money was to be split evenly among Sandy, Del, and my father, but Dad wouldn't take a nickel. My mother didn't argue about it, either, which made me think there must have been a good reason for steering clear of that cash. Aunt Sandy and Uncle Del were more than happy to take Dad's share, and they've been living the high life ever since.

'They wanted to send some hotshot Miami lawyer down to handle his case,' Mom said, 'but I told them it wasn't necessary.'

'You're right. It's not such a big deal.'

'That's not what I said, Noah. It *is* a big deal.' She scraped the chopped onion bits into a bowl, which she covered with plastic wrap and placed in the refrigerator. Later, when she was alone in the kitchen, she would empty the whole thing into the garbage.

'I'm at the end of my rope with your father,' she said.

'Mom, everything's going to work out.'

'You children need to have food on the table! The mortgage needs to be paid!' she went on angrily. 'Meanwhile he's sitting in jail, talking about fighting for his principles. He wants to be a martyr, Noah, that's fine – but not at the expense of this family. I won't stand for it!'

'Mom, I know it's a rough time—' I said, but she cut me off with a wave of her hand.

'Go clean up your room,' she said. 'Please.'

Abbey was waiting at the top of the stairs. She put a finger to her lips and led me down the hall to my parents' bedroom. She cracked open the door and pointed.

There, lying open on the bed, was my mother's suitcase. Not her vacation suitcase, either, but the big plaid one.

'Uh-oh,' I said in a whisper.

Abbey nodded gravely. 'She's serious this time, Noah. We've got to do something.'

THREE

By the time they let me visit my father again, the *Coral Queen* had been pumped dry, mopped clean, and refitted with new gambling equipment. I was hoping Dad wouldn't ask about it, but he did.

'No way!' he exclaimed when I told him that Dusty Muleman was back in action.

'They must've had twenty guys working on that boat,' I said.

My father was crushed. 'I should've taken it out and sunk it in Hawk's Channel,' he muttered, 'or the Gulf Stream.'

Luckily we were alone in the interview room. I assumed that my father had convinced the big jowly deputy – and probably everyone else at the jail – that he was harmless and fairly normal. He was good at that.

'Mom heard you might get transferred to the stockade in Key West,' I said.

'Not any more,' Dad reported in a confidential tone.

'The lieutenant here likes me. I'm teaching him how to play chess.'

'You play chess?'

'Shhhh,' my father said. 'He *thinks* I do. Hey, how's Abbey?'

'All right,' I said.

'Tell her to hang in there, Noah.'

'She says you need professional help.'

Dad sat back and chortled. 'That's our girl. Did you go see Lice Peeking?'

I described my visit to the trailer park. My father wasn't surprised that Lice turned down the old truck and wanted money in exchange for providing evidence against Dusty Muleman.

'Dad, how are we going to pay him when . . .'

'When we're flat broke? Excellent question,' my father said. 'See if Lice will take my bonefish skiff. It's worth ten or twelve grand at least.'

Secretly I'd been hoping that one day Dad would give me that boat. It was an original Hell's Bay with a sixty-horse Merc, a really sweet ride. Sometimes, late in the afternoon, my father would take me and Abbey out fishing. Even if the snappers weren't biting, we'd stay until sunset, hoping to see the green flash on the horizon. The flash was kind of a legend in the Keys – some people believed in it and some didn't. Dad claimed that he'd actually witnessed it once, on a cruise to Fort Jefferson. For our fishing expeditions either Abbey or I always brought a camera, just in case. We had a stack of pretty sunset pictures, but no green flash.

'You sure you want to give away the skiff?' I asked.

'What the heck, it's the best we can do,' Dad said.

'I guess so.' I tried not to sound too bummed.

'Hey, did you meet the famous Shelly?'

'Yeah. She's kind of scary,' I said. 'Lice said he stole her from Dusty – what did he mean exactly?'

I figured it was one of those I'll-explain-it-when-you're-older questions that my dad would brush off, but he didn't.

'Shelly was Dusty's second or third wife, after Jasper Jr's mother,' he said. Then he paused. 'Actually, maybe they were only engaged to be married. Anyway, one day she got fed up with Dusty and moved in with Lice.'

I wondered how miserable life with the Mulemans must have been to make Lice Peeking look like a prize.

'Dad, when're you coming home?' I asked.

'After the trial,' he replied.

The plan was to use his big day in court to expose Dusty Muleman's illegal polluting.

'But Mom says you can bail out and come home and still have your trial later,' I said.

'No, I need to stay here and show I'm totally committed to the cause. You know how many jails around this world are full of people who spoke up for what they believed in and lost their freedom? Lost everything they had? Look at Nelson Mandela,' my father said. 'He spent twenty-seven years in a South African prison. Twenty-seven years, Noah! A couple of weeks won't hurt me.'

'But Mom misses you,' I said.

That seemed to catch him off guard and take the steam out of his big speech. Dad looked away.

'It's a sacrifice, I know,' he said. 'I wish it didn't have to be like this.'

I didn't say anything about Mom and the plaid suitcase because she'd put it away. That morning I'd peeked in their bedroom closet – her clothes were still hanging there. So were Dad's.

When I stood up to leave, my father perked up slightly. He said, 'Oh, I almost forgot. A reporter from the *Island Examiner* might drop by the house. It's all right for you to speak with him.'

'About what?' I asked.

'My situation.'

'Oh. Sure, Dad.'

His 'situation'? I thought. Sometimes it's like my father lives on his own weird little planet.

*

In July the days get long and stream together. I try not to look at the calendar because I don't want to think about time passing. August comes way too soon, and that's when school starts in Florida.

Summer mornings are mostly sunny and still, though by mid afternoon huge boiling thunderheads start to build over the Everglades, and the weather can get interesting in a hurry. I've always liked watching the sky drop down like a foamy purple curtain when a summer storm rumbles across Florida Bay. If you're on the ocean side of the islands, it can sneak up on you from behind, which happens a lot to tourists.

That's where we were going, to Thunder Beach, when a squall rolled through after lunch. Thom, Rado, and I hunkered in the mangroves and held our skateboards over our heads, to keep the raindrops out of our eyes. It took like half an hour for the leading edge of the storm to pass. Then the wind dropped out, and the only sound was a soft sleepy drizzle.

We crawled from the tree line and brushed the leaves off our arms. Not surprisingly, the lightning had spooked everyone away from the park except us.

Before heading to the water, we scanned the shoreline for pollution warnings. Whenever the biologists from the health department find too much bacteria, they post DANGER! signs up and down Thunder Beach

– no swimming, no fishing, no anything. Only a certified moron would dive in when the beach was posted.

I was glad to see that the water was OK, especially
when a big loggerhead turtle bobbed up to the surface. The three of us stayed real quiet because we
thought the turtle might be coming ashore to lay her
eggs, although usually they waited until dark.
Loggerheads have lousy eyesight, so we were pretty
sure she didn't notice us sitting there, but she didn't
swim any closer.

We wouldn't have bothered her if she'd decided to
crawl up and dig a nest. Most of the Keys are made
of hard coral rock, and there aren't many soft beaches
like you find up the coast at Pompano or Vero. The
momma turtles down here don't have lots of options,
so we leave them alone. It's the law, too.

After the loggerhead swam off, we jumped in and
goofed around until Thom cut his ankle on a broken
beer bottle that was buried in the sand. Rado and I
helped him hop back to shore, where we tied his
Dolphins jersey around his foot to keep the cut from
getting dirty. Rado took him home while I skated
alone down the old road, back toward Lice Peeking's
place.

Nobody answered the door, and I was already down
the steps when Shelly appeared from behind the trailer
and nearly scared the you-know-what out of me. She

was barefoot and carried a long rusty shovel.

'What's you want now?' she asked. She wore cutoff jeans and a sleeveless top that showed off her barbed-wire tattoo.

'I need to talk to Mr Peeking again,' I said.

'Well, he's not available at the moment.'

'That's, OK. I'll come back another time.'

Shelly noticed me staring at the shovel. She laughed and said, 'Don't worry, it wasn't Lice I was puttin' in a hole. It was last night's dinner.'

I nodded as if that was the most normal thing in the world, burying food in your backyard.

'Lobster shells,' she explained. 'I don't want 'em stinking up the garbage, 'cause they're out of season. Next thing you know, some nosy neighbour calls the grouper troopers and then, Houston, we've got a problem.'

Some of the locals in the Keys poach a lobster here and there in the off months. Not even my dad gets upset about that.

'Whatcha wanna talk to Lice for?' Shelly asked.

'Just some business between him and my father,' I said.

She was so much taller than me, I had to tilt my head back just to see her expression. She was smiling when she said, 'Important business, huh?'

'Yes, ma'am.'

'Come on inside and have somethin' to drink.'

'No thanks. I'm soaking wet.'

'So's Lice,' Shelly grunted, 'but from the inside out.'

She jerked open the screen door and I followed her into the trailer. Lice Peeking was stretched face down on the blue shag carpet, and he wasn't moving. I didn't see any blood, which was a relief, but I couldn't hear him breathing.

Shelly said, 'Oh, don't worry. He's not dead.' She gave a sharp kick to his ribs and he started to snore.

'See?' she said. 'Tell me your name again.'

'Noah Underwood.'

'You're Paine's oldest?'

'That's right,' I said.

Shelly tossed me a Coke from the refrigerator and said, 'Your daddy's a curious specimen.' Somehow it sounded like a compliment.

I guzzled the soda in about thirty seconds while I edged toward the door. The perfume that Shelly had on was making me dizzy. It smelled like a bag of tangerines.

She sat down on a cane stool and motioned me to do the same, but I stayed on my feet. I wasn't sure what would happen if Lice Peeking woke up, and I wanted to be ready to run.

Shelly said, 'I've known Paine since back when he and Dusty used to fish charters out of Ted's. He was always a gentleman – your daddy, I mean, not Dusty.'

'Yes, ma'am.'

'How come you're actin' so skittery, Noah?'

I couldn't come out and tell her that she was the reason, that everything about her – from her face to her feet – was at least twice as big as my mother's.

So I said, 'I'm going to be late for violin practice.'

Which was incredibly lame, because we don't even own a violin. Abbey takes piano lessons on a portable electric keyboard that my father bought from a consignment shop in Key Largo.

'Now, Noah,' Shelly said, 'that's not the truth, is it?'

'No, ma'am. I'm sorry.'

'Please don't grow up to be one of those men who lie for the sport of it,' she said, 'and most men do. That's a fact.'

As Shelly spoke, she was staring down at Lice Peeking, and not in an admiring way. 'That's why the world is so messed up, Noah. That's why history books are full of so much heartache and tragedy. Politicians, dictators, kings, phoney-baloney preachers – most of 'em are men, and most of 'em lie like rugs,' she said. 'Don't you dare grow up to be like that.'

At first I thought she was making fun of me, but then realized she was serious.

'Your daddy doesn't drink, does he?' she said. 'That's truly amazing.'

It *was* sort of unusual, for the Keys. People who didn't know my father automatically assumed he had to be drunk to do some of the things he did, but he wasn't. He never touched a drop of alcohol, even on New Year's. It wasn't a religious thing; he just didn't care for the taste.

'Why can't I find a guy like that?' Shelly said in a small voice.

I couldn't help but notice that she was using Lice Peeking's head as a footrest. It didn't seem to bother him, though. He kept snoring away.

'You go to the public school?' she said. 'Then you must know Jasper Jr.'

'Sure,' I said.

'Is that boy still nasty as a pygmy rattler?'

'Nastier,' I answered honestly.

Shelly shook her head. 'He's been that way since he was about three foot high. Honestly? I don't see a bright future there.'

Her mentioning Jasper Jr reminded me of what my dad said about Shelly and Dusty Muleman, about how she'd gotten so fed up with him that she'd moved out. I decided to find out if she still felt that way.

'Didn't you used to work on the *Coral Queen*?' I asked.

'For almost three years,' said Shelly.

'Was it a fun job?'

She rolled her eyes. 'Tending bar? Oh yeah, it was a barrel of laughs. Very glamorous, too. Come on now, what're you drivin' at?'

'Nothing. I swear.'

'There you go again, Noah.'

Shelly was sharp when it came to sniffing out fibs, so I just came out and asked her: 'Did you ever hear about anything crooked going on with that boat?'

'Crooked how?' she asked.

'Like dumping sewer water into the basin.'

She laughed in a way that sounded hard and bitter. 'Sweetie,' she said, 'the only sewage I ever saw was the human kind. That's what you call the "downside" of my job.'

'Oh.'

'This has somethin' to do with your old man, doesn't it? About him sinkin' Dusty's boat?'

'Maybe.' It sounded silly as soon as I said it. 'Maybe' almost always means 'yes'.

'OK, let's hear the whole story.' Shelly cocked her head and cupped one of her ears, which had, like, five silver rings in it. 'Come on, Noah,' she said, 'I'm listening.'

There was no way I wasn't going to cave in and blab everything. She was a pro at shaking the truth out of guys who were a lot bigger and tougher than I was.

But then Lice Peeking came to the rescue. He stopped snoring, flopped over on his back, and opened one bleary red eye.

Shelly thumped him with both heels and said, 'Get up, you sorry sack of beans, before I park that slimy aquarium on your head.' I didn't wait around to see if she was serious.

FOUR

The next morning the lawyer stopped by our house. Mr Shine looked about a thousand years old, but Mom said he knew his way around the courthouse. She had hired him twice before to get my father out of trouble.

Mr Shine put his briefcase on the kitchen table and sat down. He looked mopy and grey, and his eyelids drooped. Abbey said he reminded her of Eeyore from *Winnie-the-Pooh*.

My mother made a pot of coffee and began dropping hints that Abbey and I should leave them alone. Abbey grabbed a bagel out of the toaster and ran off to play on the computer. I got my spinning rod from the garage and biked up to the drawbridge at Snake Creek.

The police won't let you fish from the top of the bridge because of the traffic, but you can go down underneath and cast from the sandbags, in the shade. Sometimes homeless people sleep under the bridges, but they usually don't bother anybody. The last time

I'd been to Snake Creek, some woman in an army jacket had made a campsite high on the bank, under the concrete braces. She'd even started a small fire, burning the wood slats from a broken stone-crab trap. I gave her a nice mangrove snapper that I caught, and she had it cleaned and cooking over the flames in five minutes flat. She said it was the best meal she'd eaten in a year. The next day Abbey and I went back with some homemade bread and a pound of fresh Gulf shrimp, but the lady was gone. I never even got her name.

On the day Mom was meeting with Mr Shine, nobody was under the bridge when I got there. The tide was running in from the ocean, and schools of finger mullet were holding in the still water behind the pilings. Every so often they'd start jumping, trying to escape some bigger fish that was prowling for lunch. I started casting a white bucktail and in no time jumped a baby tarpon that wasn't even ten pounds. Then I hooked something heavy, probably a snook, that ran out a hundred feet and broke the line.

As I was tying on another jig, I heard an outboard engine – it was a johnboat, maybe twelve feet long, motoring along Snake Creek. Two people were in the boat, and as it drew closer I recognized them as Jasper Jr and an older kid named Bull.

They spotted me right away. I probably should

have taken off, but I was really enjoying myself, fishing under that bridge. So I set down my spinning rod and watched Jasper Jr nose the johnboat into the shallows.

Bull was in the bow. He climbed out first and looped a rope around one of the pilings. He's a hefty guy, but that's not how he got his nickname – people call him Bull because you can't believe a word he says. For instance, he told everyone at school he was dropping out to play double-A ball for the Baltimore Orioles. This is at age sixteen, right? We all knew that Bull couldn't catch a pop fly if it landed in his lap, so we weren't exactly surprised to see him bagging groceries that spring at the Winn Dixie.

After Bull tied off the johnboat, he called up to me: 'Hey, buttface, better run for your life. Jasper's got a speargun!'

'Yeah, right,' I said.

When Jasper Jr hopped out of the boat, I saw that he didn't have a speargun or any other weapon. Even so, running away would have been an excellent idea. I just didn't feel like it.

Jasper Jr walked up and asked, 'What're you lookin' at?'

'Absolutely nothing,' I said with a straight face.

'I told you I was gonna find you, didn't I?'

I knew that Jasper Jr wasn't looking for me at

Snake Creek – he and Bull were heading out to poach lobsters or pull some other mischief.

But I played along. 'Well, you found me. Now what?'

That's when he socked me in the right eye. It hurt, too. Jasper Jr seemed surprised that I didn't fall down.

So was Bull. He said, 'You got a hard head, for a buttface.'

The way my cheekbone was throbbing, I figured that Jasper Jr's knuckles weren't feeling so good, either. He was trying to act like a tough guy, but I noticed that his eyes were watering from the pain. I probably could have knocked him flat, but I didn't.

My father's a large man, very strong, but he says fighting is for people who can't win with their brains. He also says there are times when you've got no choice but to defend yourself from common morons. If Jasper Jr had taken another swing at me, I definitely would have punched him back. Then Bull would have beaten me to a pulp and the whole thing would have been over.

But Jasper Jr didn't hit me again. Instead he spit in my face, which was worse in a way.

He forced a laugh and called me a couple of dirty names and headed back toward the johnboat. He was shaking the hand that he'd hit me with, as if there were a crab or a mousetrap attached to it. Bull was following behind, cackling like a hyena. They got into the boat, and Jasper Jr jerk-started the outboard while Bull shoved off from the bow.

I pulled up the front of my shirt and wiped the spit off my face. Then I grabbed my fishing rod and took aim.

The bucktail jig I happened to be using weighed one quarter of an ounce, which doesn't sound like much until it thumps you between the shoulder blades, which is where I thumped Jasper Jr. It was an awesome cast, I've got to admit. The hook on the jig snagged firmly in the mesh of Jasper Jr's ratty old basketball jersey, and he let out a howl. I gave a stiff yank and he howled again.

In a panic he twisted the throttle and the johnboat picked up speed, but that didn't help – Jasper Jr was stuck on the end of my line like a moray eel. He hollered for Bull to cut him loose, which was all right with me. I'd made my point.

Bull found a knife and clambered to the back end of the boat, which turned out to be a humungous mistake. With so much weight in the stern – Bull, Jasper Jr, plus the engine – the bow tilted upward and the johnboat began taking on water.

No sooner had Bull reached behind Jasper Jr to cut the fishing line than the motor gurgled to a dead stop. The blue-green water of Snake Creek was pouring in over the transom, but nobody in the john-boat moved. Jasper Jr was yelling at Bull and Bull was yelling back, and they just kept getting wetter and wetter. By now the motor was completely sub-merged and the bow was pointed nearly straight up in the air, which meant that the boat was about to capsize.

Bull was the first to jump, with Jasper Jr right behind him. They started swimming like maniacs toward the bumpers of the bridge, cursing the whole way. They were making such an awful racket that the mullet scattered out of the eddies, and I knew that the fishing was pretty much shot for the afternoon.

So I reeled in my line and made my way up the slope, toward the highway.

'You did *what*?' Abbey said when I told her what happened. 'Geez, you're as whacked as Dad.'

'I didn't sink their stupid boat. They sunk it themselves.'

Abbey muttered in exasperation. 'If this keeps up, we're gonna get run out of town. Mom'll have to put the house up for sale.'

'Jasper Jr spat on me,' I said.

'What happened to your eye?'

'He did that, too.'

After examining my bruise, Abbey seemed more

sympathetic. 'From now on, don't go anywhere without Thom or Rado,' she advised.

It would have been a sensible plan, except that Thom's family was heading to North Carolina for the rest of the summer, and Rado was going camping in Colorado with his mother and stepdad. Thom and Rado were my best friends, and without them I was basically on my own.

Mom came into the bedroom, and the first thing she noticed, naturally, was my black eye. I told her the whole story – Abbey hung around to make sure. My mother was real angry, but I begged her not to call Dusty Muleman and tell him what Jasper Jr had done.

'It'll just make things worse,' I said.

'What could be worse than getting punched and spat at?' she asked.

'Lots of things. Trust me, Mom.'

'Noah's right,' Abbey said.

'We'll discuss this later.' My mother's mouth wasn't moving much when she talked, which meant she was still mad. 'Noah, please go wash up. There's a gentleman waiting in the living room to speak with you.'

'Who is it?' I asked. 'Is he from the police?'

'No, from the newspaper,' Mom said, making that sound even worse. 'Apparently your father thought it would be a brilliant idea to have an article written about himself. He sent the reporter here to "interview" you.'

Abbey rolled her eyes. 'You've gotta be joking.'

'I wish I were,' said my mother. 'Hurry up, Noah, and put on a clean shirt, please. I don't want you looking like some sort of juvenile delinquent.'

'Then you ought to put some make-up on his shiner,' Abbey suggested.

'No way!' I said.

But it was too late.

The reporter's name was Miles Umlatt. He was thin and blotchy, and his nose was scuffed up like an old shoe.

Mom had stationed him on the sofa so he could set up his tape recorder on the coffee table. On his lap he held a lined yellow pad that was covered with scribbles.

I sat down in the tall armchair where my father usually sits. Mom had dabbed some flesh-coloured powder around my black eye, and she must have done a good job because Miles Umlatt didn't seem to notice. He asked what grade I was in, what sort of hobbies I enjoyed, did I own a dog or a cat – the usual stuff. He was pretending to be nice, but I could tell it was a real chore. He was dying to get to the juicy parts.

'I understand you've been to visit your father,' he said finally. 'That must've been tough.'

'Not really.' I was trying to sound kind of cool and bored.

'Yes, well, this isn't the first time your dad's had a scrape with the law, is it?'

'No, sir.'

'What do you remember about the other times?' he asked.

I just shrugged. It was amazing that Mom had left me alone in the room with this guy. I knew she was hovering somewhere nearby, but at least for now I was free to say what I wanted.

'I found an old clipping about the Carmichael family,' Miles Umlatt said. He held up the photocopy to show me.

'That was a long time ago,' I said.

'Only three years.'

'Are you sure?' I asked, although three years sounded about right.

Here's what had happened, the way my father told it: the Carmichaels drove their forty-foot, gas-hogging motor home all the way to the Keys from some place up in Michigan. They were too cheap to rent space at an RV park, so they parked along Highway One near the Indian Key Bridge and camped there for three nights.

Which would have been no big deal, except for the way they treated their dogs – they had two chocolate

Labrador retrievers that rode along with them in the motor home. One morning my dad was heading out on a tarpon-fishing charter when he spotted Mr Carmichael whipping the dogs with a bungee cord. I guess the dogs had had an accident inside the Winnebago or something. Anyhow, they were crying and yipping and trying to get away, but Mrs Carmichael (who was the size of a whale) was standing on their leashes so that Mr Carmichael could beat them.

When Dad saw that, he sort of freaked. He beached the skiff, took out his tarpon gaff, and flattened every single tyre – I think there were, like, eight of them – on the Carmichaels' RV. Then he put the two Labradors in his boat and went fishing.

The sheriff's deputies were waiting on the dock at the end of the day. My father confessed right away, as he always does, but he wouldn't apologize. He also wouldn't say what he'd done with the dogs because he knew they'd be safer away from the Carmichaels.

That time, Dad spent only two nights in jail before he let my mom bail him out. Eventually he pleaded guilty to vandalism and, I guess, dognapping, although he agreed to pay for the Labradors and a new set of Winnebago tyres. Later we found out that Dad probably would've beaten the charges because the Carmichaels had refused to come back to the Keys

47

for a trial. They wrote a letter to the judge saying that my father was a raving lunatic and they were scared to be in the same county with him, which was ridiculous.

Anyway, my dad said that running 'those puppy-whipping lowlifes' out of the islands was worth the legal hassle. A public service, is what he called it. The two chocolate Labs ended up with some friends of ours, nice people who run an Italian restaurant down in Marathon.

I listened while Miles Umlatt went through the whole story again.

'Dad just lost his temper,' I said when he was done. 'But those people were wrong. It's against the law to treat animals like that.'

Miles Umlatt wrote that down on his pad, which made me a little nervous. So did the tiny green light blinking on his tape recorder.

'Dad's just got to work on his self-control,' I added.

'Are you ever afraid of him?'

I burst out laughing, it was such a lame question.

'Afraid of my dad? You serious?'

'Well, Noah, you've got to admit,' Miles Umlatt said, 'his behaviour has been erratic. Unpredictable, I mean.'

I knew perfectly well what 'erratic' meant.

'Dad wouldn't hurt a flea,' I said firmly.

'But would he hurt a *human* who would hurt a flea?'

That's when Mom breezed in to refill Miles Umlatt's coffee cup, or at least that was her excuse.

'How's it going, fellas?' she asked.

'Just fine, Mrs Underwood,' said Miles Umlatt. 'Noah's a bright young man.'

I felt like sticking my finger down my throat. Mom flashed her fake-polite smile and said, 'Yes, we're very proud of him.'

She hung around for a while, making small talk, until the phone rang in the kitchen. As soon as we were alone again, Miles Umlatt leaned forward and said, 'Noah, what can you tell me about the incident with Derek Mays?'

'Not much.' I was sure he already knew the whole story. Everybody in the Upper Keys did. And what he didn't know he could have found out from the Coast Guard files.

'Derek says he was afraid for his life,' Miles Umlatt said.

'Maybe he was just afraid of getting busted.'

Here's what my dad said had happened: he was out bonefishing with two doctors from New Jersey when he spotted Derek Mays stringing a gill net near Little Rabbit Key. Gill nets were outlawed years ago in Florida because they kill everything that gets tangled, not just the baitfish but sharks, reds, snook, tarpon, turtles – you name it, it dies. To make things worse, the island where Derek Mays was poaching was deep in Everglades National Park, which is totally protected. Or supposed to be.

When he spotted my father, Derek hauled in the gill net and made a run for it. Dad's skiff is super quick, and it didn't take long for him to catch up. Derek refused to stop, so my father leaped right into his boat. Then it turned into a wrestling match and things got ugly. By the time the park rangers arrived, Dad had wrapped up Derek in his own net, like a big dumb mullet.

But here's the part that really got to me: not a darn thing happened to Derek because none of the rangers actually witnessed what he was doing at Little Rabbit. Meanwhile, Dad gets accused of, like, assault, and then the government takes away his captain's licence because (they said) he 'endangered' the lives of his customers by chasing after Derek at high speed. Of course, the two doctors on Dad's boat said they'd never had so much fun, but that didn't count for squat with the Coast Guard.

Which is why my father had to start driving a cab.

Miles Umlatt said, 'There seems to be a pattern to these episodes, wouldn't you say?'

'It's not like it happens every day,' I said.

The guy was definitely getting on my nerves. I was sort of annoyed at my father for choosing me to be the one for the interview. The only reason, I knew, was that Mom had refused to do it.

'Let's talk about what happened to the *Coral Queen*,' said Miles Umlatt, and he droned through *that* whole story. He told me that Dusty Muleman denied flushing polluted water from his gambling boat, which was no big surprise. Why would he ever admit to the crime?

'He threatened to sue your father for slander,' Miles Umlatt said.

'What's that?'

'Saying something bad about a person that isn't true.'

'Dad doesn't lie,' I said. 'He might do some crazy stuff, but he always tells the truth.'

'Are you proud of him, Noah?'

That was a tricky one. I wasn't proud that my dad was sitting in jail, but I knew he was a good person. Even when he flies off the handle, at least he's fighting for something close to his heart. Too many people these days, they just turn their backs or close their eyes, pretending everything is wonderful in the world. Well, it's not.

'I am proud of my father,' I said to Miles Umlatt, 'for standing up for what he believes. But, like I said, once in a while he goes too far.'

Miles Umlatt jotted down every word. 'Your dad said he considers himself a political prisoner. Would you agree with that?'

Political prisoner? I thought. Give me a break. I knew Mom wasn't eavesdropping, because she would have blown a fuse.

'I don't know much about politics,' I said carefully, 'but he's definitely a prisoner.'

Miles Umlatt seemed to think that was very funny. He wrote it down, closed his notebook, and switched off his tape recorder.

'Thank you, Noah. That was perfect,' he said. Then he shook my hand and skittered out the front door.

My mother was still on the phone in the kitchen. She gave me a thumbs-up signal when I came in to grab some cookies. On the way to my room I stopped outside Abbey's doorway and listened. She was crying, which got me worried because my sister hardly ever cries.

I opened the door to check on her. She was sitting on the edge of the bed with a box of Kleenex on her lap and a pile of pink crumpled-up tissues on the floor. I could tell she was really upset because she didn't holler at me for barging in without knocking.

'What's wrong?' I asked.

'It's Mom,' she sniffled.

'But I just saw her. She seemed OK.'

Abbey shook her head. 'That lawyer. Sh-Sh-Shine.' She was trying to catch her breath between sobs.

'What about him? He won't take Dad's case?'

'W-w-worse,' Abbey stammered. 'I heard Mom ask him . . .'

Here she paused to snatch another tissue and dab at her eyes.

'Ask him what?' I said impatiently.

'She d-d-didn't know I was standing by the d-d-door.'

'Abbey, it's all right. Calm down, OK?'

'OK.' She straightened up and swallowed hard, and for a moment she looked like her old brave self.

'Now tell me,' I said, 'what was Mom asking Mr Shine about?'

'The d-word,' my sister whispered.

'Divorce?'

Abbey nodded. Her lower lip began to tremble, and her shoulders went kind of slack, so I sat on the bed and put one arm around her and tried to act stronger than I felt.

FIVE

Everybody was quiet at breakfast the next morning. Mom said she was taking Abbey shopping. I told her I was going fishing again, which was a possibility.

First, though, I had to have another talk with my father. I wanted him to know that Mom had mentioned the d-word – surely *that* would shake him up enough to come home.

As soon as Mom and Abbey left, I got on my bike and headed up the highway toward the jail. I wasn't sure they'd let me in without Mom calling to arrange it, so I brought along a letter that had arrived for my father at the house. It was from the US State Department, and the seal on the envelope made it look very important.

I already knew what the letter said because my mother had opened it. The government was telling us (for about the fifteenth time) that the body of Robert Lee Underwood, my Grandpa Bobby, was still down in Colombia. They couldn't bring him home because there was a problem with the paperwork, and the police in the village 'were not responding to enquiries from the United States Embassy'. The news wasn't going to cheer up Dad, but at least it gave me an excuse to see him again.

When I showed the envelope to the deputy at the desk, he didn't seem very impressed. He peeked inside to make sure that it was only a letter, and he said he'd give it to my father later.

'Can't I give it to him myself?' I asked.

'No, he's busy this morning,' the deputy said.

Busy? I thought. Doing what – pretending to play chess?

'Is he all right?' I said.

The deputy chuckled. 'Yeah, he's fine. There's a TV crew that drove down from Miami to see him.'

'TV?'

'Yeah, Channel Ten. They said they'll need at least an hour.'

'Then I'll come back later,' I said.

The deputy shook his head. 'Sorry, sport. Inmates are allowed only one short visit per day, and we're already bending the rules for this TV thing. Maybe tomorrow you can see your old man. But call first, OK?'

Sure enough, there was a shiny new van from Channel 10 parked outside the sheriff's station. I don't know why I hadn't noticed it before. I rode away wondering how to tell my mother that Dad was now doing television interviews from jail. She'd find out sooner or later, when it was on the news, because all the Miami TV stations broadcast to the Keys.

So I'd have to tell her, even though she wouldn't be happy about it. Maybe Dad thought of himself as a political prisoner, but Mom thought he was being a selfish jerk.

Lice Peeking was actually awake and semi-alert when I stopped at the trailer. Shelly wasn't there, which was sort of a relief and a disappointment at the same time. She made me real nervous – but she also kept Lice Peeking from acting up.

'Well, lookie who's here,' he said with a wormy smile.

He was lounging on the front stoop, sucking on a cigarette. His hair was wet and tangly, and his shirt was damp. I couldn't tell whether he'd taken a shower or sprayed himself down with a garden hose.

'So, how's the jailbird?' he asked.

'Oh, that's real funny.' I didn't appreciate him talking that way about Dad. It was different when Abbey did it because she was family. Lice Peeking was just a lazy lump who didn't know anything about my father.

'Well, what'd he say?' Lice Peeking asked. 'Can he come up with some money or not?'

I said, 'We don't have any money, but he'll give you his flats skiff. It's worth twelve thousand dollars.'

Lice Peeking squinted one bloodshot eye. 'Says who?'

'Come see for yourself. It's on a trailer behind our house.' I told him what kind of boat it was, and that the engine had fewer than a hundred hours on it.

'Seriously?' he said.

'My father doesn't lie.'

'And it's free and clear, this boat? The bank don't own a piece?'

'Dad paid off the loan last year,' I said.

Lice Peeking scratched his chin, which was raw and peeling. 'Where's your house at?' he asked.

I gave him directions. It nearly broke my heart to think of a loser like that taking our skiff and selling it for cash. But what else could we do?

Lice Peeking flicked his cigarette butt under the trailer and pulled himself upright. 'Let's go have a look,' he said, which caught me by surprise.

'It's a long way to walk,' I said.

'Who's walkin', boy?' He laughed and pointed at my bicycle. 'Hop up on the handlebars.'

And that's what I did.

It had been a while since Lice Peeking had pedalled a bike, and he was wheezing by the time we got to the house. He seemed shocked that there was no beer in the refrigerator, but he settled for a Diet Coke. We went out back to see Dad's skiff, and Lice Peeking made up his mind right away. It was a cool-looking boat.

'We definitely got us a deal,' he said. 'I'll be back with Shelly and the Jeep to pick it up – say tomorrow 'round noon?'

'Hold on,' I said. 'It's not free.'

Lice Peeking sniffed. 'Chill out, junior, I know that.'

'My dad wants you to sign a statement telling what you saw when you worked on the *Coral Queen*. You know, about Mr Muleman making them empty the dirty holding tank into the water.'

'Sure, no sweat,' Lice Peeking said.

'And anything else illegal you know about. Like, if they're dumping garbage or oil, too. You need to write it all down.'

'You bet.' He was walking back and forth, admiring the skiff from different angles. 'Now, the trailer's included, right?'

'Yes, sir,' I said. 'Could you please bring the statement when you come get the boat?'

Lice Peeking made a face and looked down at me. 'You want it tomorrow? Seriously?'

'Yes, sir. And Dad says it's got to be signed and witnessed,' I told him. 'That's the deal.'

'Geez, you're quite the young hardass, ain't ya?'

'No, sir,' I said. 'My father's in jail and I want to help him out. That's all.'

On the way back to the trailer court we passed Jasper Muleman Jr and Bull pushing a wheelbarrow down the bike path. It was obviously a strain, and as we rode past I saw why. Balanced upside down in the wheelbarrow was the mud-splattered outboard motor from the johnboat that had sunk in Snake Creek. The engine's propeller was dented and caked with greenish crud.

Jasper Jr called out something nasty as we rode by, but I was surprised when Lice Peeking braked the bicycle and spun around. I told him to forget about it, just keep going, but he was mad. He pedalled straight up to Jasper Jr and Bull, blocking their path.

'What was that you just said, boy?' Lice Peeking demanded.

'I wasn't talkin' to you,' Jasper Jr mumbled.

'He was talking to *me*. Honest,' I said to Lice Peeking. I didn't want any trouble right there on the main highway, where everybody could see us.

But Lice Peeking didn't let up.

'Sounds like you got your daddy's potty mouth,' he said to Jasper Jr. 'Keep it up, you'll need a whole new setta choppers before you're eighteen.'

Bull said, 'Come on, Lice, he didn't mean nothin'. That's the truth.'

'Shut up, Bull,' said Lice Peeking. 'You wouldn't know the truth if it stung you on the butt. Now, Jasper, how 'bout you apologize to me and my friend?'

I could have gone my whole entire life without Lice Peeking calling me his 'friend'. On the inside I was cringing.

Jasper Jr shot me a vicious glare. Then he turned sulky and looked down at his feet.

'I'm waitin', boy,' said Lice Peeking.

'I'll 'polgize to you,' Jasper Jr said finally, 'but not to him.'

He jerked his grimy chin toward me.

Bull blurted, 'Underwood's old man sunk Jasper's pappy's boat!'

'Like I care,' Lice Peeking said.

He placed one boot on the rim of the wheelbarrow and gave a push. It turned over sideways, toppling the outboard motor with a crunch onto the hard asphalt. A gush of oily grey fluid spilled from the cracked cowling.

Bull groaned. Jasper Jr's jaw fell open.

'Don't call people names,' Lice Peeking said. 'It ain't polite.'

Then we rode away.

That night, after dinner, Mom put on a CD by a singer named Sheryl Crow. One of the songs was called 'My

Favourite Mistake', and my mother liked to joke that she could have written it herself – about my dad.

This time, though, she didn't smile when the song came on.

I was going to tell her about Dad doing that interview with Channel 10, but I decided to wait until she was in a better mood. I didn't tell my sister, either, because she'd get ticked off and start throwing stuff around her room. Abbey has a hot temper.

Around ten-fifteen Mom turned off the stereo, gave me a hug, and went off to bed. I was pretty tired, but I stayed up reading a skateboard magazine and kept one eye on the clock. At exactly midnight I crept down the hall and tapped on Abbey's door. She was wide awake and ready to go. We snuck out through the kitchen and got our bicycles from the garage.

It didn't take long to reach the marina. The *Coral Queen* had just closed and the passengers were filing off, laughing and talking loudly. Abbey and I hid nearby, on one of the deep-sea charter boats. We crouched low in the stern so that nobody could see us.

A yellow crescent moon peeked out from behind the clouds, and the mosquitoes weren't too bad. We just sat there not saying a word, looking up at the sky and waiting for the docks to quiet down. By the time all the gamblers were gone, we could hear the jacks and tarpon crashing schools of minnows in the basin.

When I peered over the gunwale, I spotted Dusty Muleman's big black Escalade parked under one of the lampposts near the *Coral Queen*. The sound of men's voices carried across the still water, and I could see figures moving around on the casino boat. My sister got on her knees beside me.

'How long you want to wait here?' she asked anxiously. 'Mom's gonna freak if she wakes up and we're gone.'

I checked my watch: ten minutes after one. 'We'll give it to one-thirty,' I said, 'then we'll go home.'

The way Dad had explained it, big boats like the *Coral Queen* are supposed to pump their toilet waste from onboard holding tanks into a sealed vat onshore. Later a sewage truck collects the stuff and hauls it to a treatment plant.

Dad believed that Dusty Muleman's boat was flushing hundreds of gallons of poop directly into the basin, which is not only gross (as Abbey would say) but also a big-time crime. All we had to do was catch him in the act and call the coast guard to come arrest him.

Then everybody in town would know that my father wasn't some kind of loony troublemaker, that he was just a guy who cared about the kids and the beaches and the things that lived in the sea. And when the truth about Dusty came out and everyone saw that Dad was right, Mom would feel better about staying married to him.

Maybe we were kidding ourselves, but that's how Abbey and I had it figured.

So we both got excited when we noticed the workers dragging a long thick hose toward the stern of the *Coral Queen*. We were sure – I mean, one thousand per cent certain – that they'd open the valve and drop the end of that hose into the water.

But they didn't. They snaked it over to the dock and connected it to something that resembled a giant rust-freckled egg.

'Hey,' whispered Abbey, 'that looks like a sewer tank.'

'Yeah, it does.' There was a knot in my stomach. I couldn't believe what we were seeing.

'What if Dad made a mistake?' she asked gloomily. 'What if Dusty's totally legal? What if the pollution is coming from somewhere else?'

I had no answer. It had never occurred to me that my father might have blamed the wrong person.

'What do we do now?' Abbey said.

'I really don't know.'

'Noah?'

'Abbey, I said I *don't know*.'

'Noah!'

From the hitch in her voice, I sensed something was wrong. I turned and saw, in the pale glow of the marina lights, a thick greasy arm around my little sister's neck.

SIX

When Abbey was a baby, she had a nasty habit that nearly drove us nuts. Even in the hottest part of summer we'd have to put on long clothes to protect our arms and legs – and forget about having company over. It was too dangerous.

My sister was a biter.

Not that she was a mean little kid; she just liked to chew. My dad called her a pit bull in diapers. In those days she'd gnaw on just about anything, and I don't mean 'nibble'. When Abbey chomped, she chomped hard. One time she crunched on a marble like it was a gumball.

So I had a hunch what was about to happen on the deep-sea boat when the bald crooked-nosed guy grabbed my sister around her neck. I could see her eyeing the meaty part of his forearm, and I thought: Whoever this goon is, some major pain is headed his way.

The instant Abbey clamped down, the stranger howled and let loose of her neck. Abbey herself didn't let go so quickly. The stranger screamed and thrashed and flapped his arm until finally he shook free. He was rearing back to smack her when I socked him, a kidney shot to the lower back, and he dropped to one knee. I snatched my sister by the sleeve and together we jumped from the deck.

We hit the dock running and never looked back. The bald guy was swearing so loudly that it carried clear across the water into the mangroves. We grabbed our bikes from the woods, and I never pedalled so fast in my life. Abbey was close behind, spitting and spluttering to get the stranger's germs out of her mouth.

When we got to our street, we had another scare. There was a light on in the house.

'Mom's bedroom,' my sister said with a groan. 'We're toast.'

'Maybe not. Maybe she's just reading a book.'

'Yeah, right,' Abbey said. 'So what's our story going to be?'

I knew we couldn't come up with a clever excuse for slipping out so late – nothing that would fool my mother, that was for sure.

'No story,' I decided. 'We'll tell her the truth.'

'Great plan, Noah. Except, how about *you* tell her? I'll be hiding in the closet, in case she goes ballistic.'

We walked our bikes to the house and propped them against the trunk of a gumbo limbo. The back door was still unlocked, the way we'd left it, which was a good sign.

Abbey went inside first and I followed, half expecting to be ambushed. My father says Mom has eyes like a hawk and ears like a panther. The odds of sneaking by her twice in one night without getting nabbed were slim.

Yet there wasn't a peep as we tiptoed past Mom and Dad's room. I went straight to bed, while Abbey spent like ten minutes gargling and brushing her teeth. I couldn't believe the racket she was making – she sounded like a duck swallowing a harmonica. Mom would've had to be in a coma not to hear it.

Still, her door never opened.

LOCAL CABBIE DEFENDS SINKING OF CASINO BOAT

That was the headline the next morning in the *Island Examiner*. The paper lay open on the breakfast table, and it was clear from my mother's expression that she'd already read the story.

'How bad is it?' I asked.

'Well, you came off like a sensible young man,' she replied. 'Your father, however, is now comparing himself to Nelson Mandela.'

'Uh-oh.'

'He's even talking about a hunger strike.'

'No way.'

'Here. See for yourself.' Mom slid the newspaper across the table.

I forced myself to read the article from beginning to end. Miles Umlatt obviously thought my father was quite a character. He'd let Dad go on and on about greedy polluters, and he'd put in the stuff about what happened with Derek Mays and the Carmichaels. Miles Umlatt described my father as 'passionate about the environment' but also 'volatile and impulsive'. That part was pretty accurate, I had to admit.

The story included a couple of quotes from me – one was about Dad needing to work on his self-control, and the other was about how he wouldn't hurt a flea. It was weird seeing my own words in print. They didn't look the same in the newspaper as they'd sounded when I'd said them out loud into Miles Umlatt's tape recorder.

Mom noticed I wasn't overjoyed with how the article had turned out. 'It's all right, Noah,' she said. 'You told the truth – your dad's a peaceful, well-meaning guy who occasionally loses a wing nut. Anybody who reads that story can see how much you care.'

'It's not just what I said, Mom. It's all the other junk in there, too.' Above the article was my father's mug shot from the day he was arrested, and also a picture of the *Coral Queen* after she had sunk.

'Half the article is Dusty Muleman saying Dad's a liar and a crackpot,' I said.

'Dusty plays golf every Sunday with the newspaper's publisher,' my mother said. 'Besides, the man's got a right to defend himself. Your father's made some serious accusations.'

Accusations that might even be false, I thought, remembering what we'd seen at the dock the night before.

Mom poured me a bowl of cereal and a tall glass of milk but I wasn't very hungry. Abbey stumbled into the kitchen looking as if she'd gotten maybe two hours of sleep. She was rubbing her eyes with one hand and trying to get a snarl out of her hair with the other. Mom and I knew better than to start a conversation – even at her best, my sister wasn't a bundle of cheer in the mornings.

She snatched up the *Island Examiner* and sped through Miles Umlatt's article, grumbling the whole time.

'Hunger strike!' she huffed when she was done, slapping the newspaper on the table. 'What's wrong with him? Is he dense or what?'

'Abbey, don't talk that way about your father,' Mom said, 'and the word is "deluded", not dense.'

'But this is so embarrassing. Can't he understand

that?' She slumped into a chair and laid her head on her arms.

'How about some scrambled eggs?' my mother asked.

'Ack!' said Abbey.

I excused myself and hurried out the door.

The scene at the jail wasn't as laid back as before. At the door a deputy actually frisked me, like you see on TV. All I'd brought was a paperback book about chess – I figured my father ought to learn the game for real, before the lieutenant figured out he was faking it. The deputy examined the puny little chess book as if he was expecting to find a false compartment and a skeleton key. When he finally returned it to me, he announced that the visitation time had been cut to five minutes, on orders from the sheriff himself.

I waited a long while in the interview room. The big jowly deputy was there, too, but he stared right through me. When my father eventually came out, he was wearing a faded orange jumpsuit with the words MONROE COUNTY INMATE stamped on the back.

'Nice fit,' I said.

'Oh, they're just ticked off at me because of the newspaper story. Did you see it?' he asked.

'Oh yeah. So did Mom and Abbey.'

'And?'

'Nobody's buying the hunger strike,' I told him, 'and you definitely need to back off this Mandela thing.'

Dad seemed disappointed at the family's reaction to the *Island Examiner* article, but I couldn't lie to him.

'You need to come home. Seriously,' I said.

'Noah, please don't start with that again.'

I gave him the chess book. He winked and said thanks.

'You seen Mom?' I asked.

'Not in a few days. I know she's been real busy with work.' He shook off the question, like it was no big deal.

'Haven't you talked to her on the phone?'

'I've tried to call, but the machine always picks up.'

I could see that my father was concerned, which was healthy. When it came to Mom, he needed to be. It's pathetic for grown-ups to pretend everything's OK when it's not.

'Listen, Dad, there's something you need to know.' I lowered my voice, as if it mattered. The room was so tiny that the deputy could hear me blink.

'We snuck down to the dock last night after the *Coral Queen* closed,' I said. 'We hid aboard one of the charter boats.'

'Who hid – not you and Abbey?'

'Yes, me and Abbey.'

I didn't dare tell Dad about the stranger grabbing my sister, because I knew he'd bail himself out of jail in a flash and go hunting for the guy. In no time he'd be back in the slammer, for doing something even worse.

'Guess what?' I said. 'Dusty's crew didn't pump the waste water into the basin. They hooked up to a sewer tank onshore.'

At first Dad was stunned. 'You sure?'

'We saw it with our own eyes,' I said.

My father rubbed his jaw and made a faint clicking sound with his teeth. 'You know what it is? Dusty's freaking out because of all the publicity about me sinking his stupid boat. He's going to lay low and act like a model citizen, in case the coast guard comes snooping around.'

It was possible, for sure. But if Dusty Muleman was starting to obey the law, I thought, how would we ever prove that Dad's accusations were right?

As if reading my thoughts, he said, 'Lice Peeking knows the truth about the *Coral Queen*. What'd he say about my skiff? Will he take it or not?'

'He's picking it up at noon.'

'Excellent!'

'And he promised to sign a statement, like you wanted.'

'Noah, that's super!'

Dad slapped me a high five. I didn't want to spoil his mood by reminding him that Lice Peeking wasn't the most reliable human being on the island. Obviously my father had let his hopes go sky-high, but since I wasn't the one sitting in jail, I kept my mouth shut.

'Time's up,' the jowly deputy said to me. He jerked his head toward the door.

'Everything's gonna work out just dandy,' my father said. 'You're doing a great job, son, but no more sneaking around at night – especially with your sister. You hear me?'

He stood up and tucked the chess book under his arm. The orange jumpsuit had no pockets – I guess the sheriff didn't want prisoners carrying anything that couldn't be seen.

'Oh, I almost forgot,' Dad said. 'Channel Ten is running my interview tonight on the five o'clock news! Be sure to tell your mom.'

'Cool,' I said, though I was seriously tempted to rush home and break the television.

After lunch I sat down under a tamarind tree and waited for Lice Peeking. I had a story ready for when Mom asked me why he was taking the skiff. I planned to tell her that Dad was loaning it out for a few weeks.

The truth was more complicated, and Mom wouldn't have approved.

After an hour or so I got restless. I walked around to the backyard and climbed up the trailer and sat down in the skiff. I started thinking about all the great times we'd had – Dad, Abbey, and me – on our sunset trips. My mother wasn't keen on fishing, but she was always happy when we'd come back with a cooler full of snappers. Abbey said Mom was just relieved that we'd gotten home in one piece, but I think it was more than that. Mom really loved it when we were doing things together – she and Abbey fixing the salad and potatoes, Dad and me cleaning the fish.

Those nights are the best times ever. My mother's always waiting on the front stoop when we pull into the driveway, and the first question she asks is: 'Did you see the green flash?' Abbey says Mom's only kidding, but I think she really believes in it.

And my father always gives her the same answer. 'Maybe next time,' he says, 'but it won't happen, Donna, unless you come along.'

But she usually doesn't. The skiff is kind of small for all four of us.

After a while Abbey came outside and hopped in the boat with me. I told her that Lice Peeking was late.

'Maybe he chickened out,' she said.

'For twelve thousand dollars? No way.'

'Maybe Dusty Muleman offered him more if he kept his mouth shut.'

Leave it to my sister to think of something like that. From what I'd seen of Lice Peeking, I didn't think he'd sneak back to Dusty in hopes of a better deal. Lice had seemed perfectly satisfied with the idea of taking Dad's boat and selling it.

'He's probably still working on his statement,' I said.

'Or his hangover,' said Abbey.

'Maybe I'd better go check on him.'

'I'll come with you.'

'No, Abbey, you need to stay here in case he shows up for the boat.' More important, I didn't want her to see Lice Peeking passed out drunk in that smelly trailer, if that's where he was.

'If you're not back in an hour,' my sister said, 'I'm either telling Mom or calling the cops.'

'Whatever,' I said. One was just as bad as the other.

I grabbed my bike and headed full speed down the old road. I'd had a bad feeling about Lice Peeking from the beginning, and now it looked like I might be right. If he was Dad's best hope for a witness against Dusty Muleman, we might be in deep trouble.

Halfway to the trailer park it started pouring, and I was drenched by the time I got there. I knocked so hard that the door swung open.

Dripping like a dog, I stepped inside. The TV was blaring – some station that shows country-music videos all day long. I turned it off and called out, 'Helloooo?'

Nothing.

'Anybody home? Mr Peeking?'

From the rear of the trailer came a muffled *thump-thump* of footsteps, and I tensed up. I was ready to run if Lice came out bombed or acting crazy.

But it was Shelly who walked up the hall, all alone. She looked red in the cheeks and not very happy. She was wearing the top half of a blue bathing suit and a Hawaiian-style wraparound skirt. Her brassy blonde hair was pinned in a bun, and she was limping. I noticed that her right foot was wrapped in tape, and I wondered if it had something to do with the base-ball bat she was carrying.

'Sorry for barging in,' I said, taking a backward step toward the door. 'I knocked for a long time but nobody heard me.'

'I was busy redecorating. What do you want?'

'Mr Peeking was supposed to stop over today and look at my dad's bonefish boat.'

'And he didn't show up? My darlin' Lice? What a surprise.' Shelly laughed in a cold way that made me shudder.

'Is he here?' I asked.

'Nope.'

'Do you know where I could reach him?'

'Nope.'

For several moments we stood there not saying anything, the rain drumming on the aluminium roof.

'What happened to your foot?' I heard myself ask.

'I believe I busted it,' Shelly replied.

'How?'

'Kicking the toilet to death.'

'Oh,' I said.

'I was pretending it was Lice's butt. He's gone, by the way, in case you hadn't figured that out.'

'Gone where?'

'Wherever it is that gutless, lazy, lowlife boyfriends go,' she said. 'Bolted last night while I was in the shower. Took my Jeep, too. The cops found it abandoned this morning up near the toll plaza at Cutler Ridge.'

I didn't know what to say, but I had to be careful. Shelly looked like she was aching to use that baseball bat.

'But Mr Peeking told me he doesn't have a driver's licence,' I said.

'A minor technicality,' said Shelly, 'for a weasel like him. Have a seat, Noah.'

'I really better be going.'

'I said *have a seat*.'

So I did.

'Some man came by to see Lice last night,' she said, 'just before he ran off. A big bald-headed guy with a weird foreign accent – French or Russian or something.'

'He was bald?' I thought of the stranger who'd grabbed Abbey at the marina.

'Like a bowling ball,' Shelly said. 'Plus, he looked like somebody gave him a nose job with a socket wrench. Lice went outside to talk, and he came back white as a ghost. Wouldn't tell me anything, either. Waited until I was in the shower, then he took off. Did I mention he grabbed all the cash?'

'No, ma'am.'

'A hundred and eighty-six bucks. Everything I had.'

'That stinks.' I felt queasy, like somehow it was all my fault.

'Funny,' Shelly said, 'but Lice didn't say nothin' about buyin' your daddy's boat.'

'I've really got to go now.'

'Remember what I told you about lying, Noah?'

'Yes, ma'am.'

'Besides, you can't be out in this rain. You'll catch strep.'

I was more than ready to risk it. 'Please,' I said. 'My mom's gonna be worried.'

Shelly nodded toward the telephone. 'Then give her a jingle.'

Of course, I didn't move.

Shelly smiled. 'Tell me about Lice and your daddy's boat,' she said. 'Tell me everything, OK? I'm sure it won't take long.'

I couldn't take my eyes off the wooden bat, which she was slapping from one palm to the other.

'Relax, kid, this isn't for you,' she said.

I wasn't taking any chances. Without hesitating, I told her all about the secret deal between my father and Lice Peeking. I figured she'd just laugh and tell me I was stupid for trusting her no-good boyfriend, but I was wrong.

What she said was: 'Noah, I think I can help you.'

Which was the last thing I expected.

SEVEN

The speeding ticket that my mother had been waiting in line to pay when she met my father was the only one she's ever gotten. She isn't a person who breaks the law, no matter how small the law might be. Most of the time Mom is steady, careful, and totally in control – in other words, the polar opposite of my dad.

Like him, she was born in Florida – a place called Kissimmee, up near Orlando. Both her parents worked as performers at Disney World, which sounds like more fun than it was. Grandpa Kenneth was Pluto, the cartoon dog, while Grandma Janet played one of Snow White's seven dwarfs – either Sleepy or Grumpy, I forget which. Mom still has a framed photograph of her mother and father dressed in costume, standing with their heads off in front of Cinderella's Castle.

According to Mom, Grandpa Kenneth didn't like his job from day one. The Pluto outfit was top-heavy and hard to navigate, and the temperature inside was about 105 degrees. The tourist kids would poke

Grandpa Kenneth in the ribs and pinch his nose and yank on his floppy ears, but he wasn't allowed to say a word. That's because Goofy is the only Disney dog character who talks – Pluto just whines or yips. So when the kids started hassling Grandpa Kenneth, all he could do was bark or shake his head or wag his paw, which almost never worked.

One day he just 'snapped'. That's Mom's word for what happened. Some brat yanked one too many times on his tail, and Grandpa Kenneth spun around and punted him halfway down Main Street USA. The kid's family sued Disney World for some insane amount of money, but by then Grandpa Kenneth and Grandma Janet had already packed up and moved to Moose Lick, Saskatchewan, where they opened a snowmobile dealership and never laid eyes on another tourist. We've gone up to visit them two or three times, but they refuse to come down to the Keys. Grandpa Kenneth is sure that the Disney people will have him arrested if he ever sets foot in Florida.

My mother returned when she was eighteen, to attend college at the state university in Gainesville. She was on her way to becoming a lawyer when she met a guy and got married and dropped out of school. The guy turned out to be a 'knucklehead' (Mom's word again), and after only two years she pulled the plug. She was driving to the courthouse with the divorce papers when she got the speeding ticket that led to her meeting my father. They got married the day after her divorce was final.

Whenever Dad starts telling that story, my mother goes out to stack the dishes or fold the laundry. She doesn't like anyone bringing up her first marriage in front of us. I know that Dad's crazy for my mom, but sometimes he's totally clueless about her feelings. Abbey gets frustrated and tells me to talk some sense into him, but what am I supposed to say?

Better shape up, Dad. Remember what happened to the last knucklehead she married.

Even if I said something, he wouldn't take it seriously. He'd tell me not to worry because Mom was his 'biggest fan'. My father has a bad habit of overestimating his charm – and also my mother's patience.

When I got back from the trailer park, she was standing in the driveway and talking with Mr Shine, the lawyer. I waved and hurried inside the house, where Abbey was waiting to fill me in.

'I was right!' she said. 'They're going to ask a judge to decide if Dad's a certified wacko.'

'But he's not,' I protested.

'The point is to get him out of jail, even if he doesn't want to leave,' said Abbey. 'The judge can order him released so he can get tested by some shrinks. That's the new plan.'

'Does Mom really think Dad's a nutcase?'

'Noah, you're missing the big picture.'

'Did she tell you all this, or were you spying on her and Mr Shine?'

'No comment,' my sister whispered. 'The good news is, I didn't hear the d-word. Not even once.'

'Excellent.' I decided not to mention that Mom and Mr Shine had gotten real quiet when they saw me riding up the driveway.

'So what did Lice Peeking have to say?' Abbey asked. 'Or was he crashed out on the floor again?'

'He wasn't even home.'

'I was right, huh? He chickened out on the deal.'

'His girlfriend thinks he skipped town,' I admitted, 'but she promised to help us nail Dusty Muleman.'

'Oh, please,' my sister sighed. 'Earth to Noah: it's a lost cause.'

'No, Abbey, it's not.'

She eyed me closely. 'You're not done with bad news, are you? I can tell.'

All I could do was shrug. 'Dad's going to be on TV tonight.'

'Why? For what?'

'He gave an interview to Channel Ten at the jail.'

'Oh, brilliant,' Abbey said, and sank into a chair. She and I were worried about the same thing: what would Mom do when she saw my father on the five o'clock news?

'How much does a new television cost?' my sister asked.

'Too much. I already thought of that.'

'A baseball would do the job,' she said. 'I could tell Mom I was tossing it around the living room when it accidentally-on-purpose hit the TV screen. I'll take all the blame. Come on, Noah, how about it?'

'I've got a better idea,' I said.

One that wasn't so messy.

Shortly before the news was supposed to come on, a hideous scream arose from my sister's room. Even though I knew she was faking it, Abbey's yowling still gave me goose bumps. She could make a fortune doing horror movies if she wanted.

While Mom went running to see what was wrong, I slipped out the kitchen door. I grabbed my fishing rod from the garage and dashed to the corner of the house where Dad had mounted the TV satellite dish. It took me only three casts to snag it with the bucktail. I jerked hard, and I kept on pulling until the dish rotated toward me. Then I clamped down on the spool of the spinning reel and backed up until the line snapped.

When I went back inside, there was Abbey sniffling on the couch in the living room. Mom sat beside her, pressing an ice pack to the back of her head.

'She fell off her bed,' Mom reported sympathetically.

'Is that all?' I said. 'It sounded like she was being boiled alive.'

'Noah!' Mom scolded, and instantly my sister started bawling again. Abbey can cry at the drop of a hat. I avoided making eye contact because I knew we'd both break up laughing.

At five o'clock Mom reached for the remote control to turn on the news, but there was no picture on the television screen – only ripples and fuzz. Mom switched to another station, and it looked the same.

'What's wrong with the set?' she muttered, and began clicking through the channels.

When I snuck a peek at Abbey, she gave me a congratulatory wink. The TV wasn't working because the satellite dish was no longer pointed up at the satellites. It was pointed at the ground.

Eventually I'd have to explain how one of my fishing lures got hooked on the dish, but for the moment I was proud of myself for sparing my mother from seeing my jailbird father on the Channel 10 news.

That good feeling lasted only a few minutes, and then our phone started ringing. Apparently everybody else on the island had watched Dad's big interview, and many of them wanted to share their reactions with Mom, who was mortified. At least three of her so-called friends had even videotaped the show, and one of them stopped by after dinner to drop off the cassette.

Abbey and I were curious about what my father had said on TV, but neither of us was brave enough to sit up with Mom while she watched the tape. I'd thought about trying to mess up the VCR, but Abbey said it would be a waste of time. She was probably right – Mom was determined to see Dad's interview, one way or another.

So my sister and I retreated to our rooms. I couldn't get to sleep, so I sat up playing my Game Boy and reading skateboard magazines. At one in the morning I was surprised to hear the telephone ring, and someone picked up right away. When I peeked down the hall, I saw that the whole house was dark except for a light in my mother's room, just like the night before.

This time, though, I could hear her voice. She was talking with Grandma Janet up in Canada. I couldn't make out everything Mom was saying, but I heard enough to know that she wasn't impressed by Dad's performance on television.

What I also heard, too clearly, was the d-word.

I'm not scared to be out alone at night. Actually, I enjoy the peace and quiet. Sometimes I sneak away from the house and ride down to Thunder Beach, or

Whale Harbour. The main things to watch for are drunk drivers and, of course, police cars. It's unusual to see a kid on a bicycle after midnight, so the cops automatically figure that you're either running away from home or out stealing stuff. More than once I've had to lay down my bike and duck into some trees when a police cruiser went by.

Mom was still on the phone when I went out the back door. On the way to the marina I didn't see a single car – a Greyhound bus was the only thing that passed me on the highway.

The *Coral Queen* was dark and the docks were quiet, but I didn't take any chances. I left my bicycle in the mangroves and checked out the place on foot. It was a good thing I did, too. The crooked-nosed bald guy who'd grabbed Abbey was sitting in a beat-up old station wagon, parked beside Dusty Muleman's ticket office.

I crouched behind the sewage tank and watched him for several minutes. He never moved even slightly, and when I edged closer, I could hear him snoring. He sounded just like Rado's dog, Godzilla, when he sleeps.

Finally I got up my nerve and crept past him. That turned out to be the easy part. Getting off the *Coral Queen* was a different story.

I'd been rummaging through the wheelhouse,

hunting for any scrap of evidence that might help Dad – a note in the crew's log, an order in Dusty's handwriting to dump the tanks, whatever – when a mullet boat rumbled into the basin. A man in rubber boots rose in the bow and started tossing a cast net. The noise woke up the bald guy, who got out of the car and stretched his arms and lit up a cigarette.

Now I was stuck. There was no way to leave the *Coral Queen* without being spotted under the dock lights. I could see Dusty's goon guy sitting on the hood of his station wagon, the tip of the cigarette glowing orange whenever he took a drag.

On tiptoes I made my way down a stairwell to the second casino deck, which, like the others, was enclosed to keep out the rain. I snooped around until I found a rack of poker chips that the crew had forgotten to lock away. I carried the rack up toward the front of the boat and opened one of the side windows. I waited there until the mullet netter motored out of the basin and the marina was quiet.

Then I reached out the window and dropped the poker-chips. They made a very impressive racket, clattering on the hard deck and rolling in a hundred directions.

The bald watchman tossed his cigarette, slid off the hood of the station wagon, and headed for the *Coral Queen*. He was bounding up the aft stairs as I was sneaking down the forward stairs. When I heard his heavy footsteps on the deck above me, I hustled to the stern, stepped lightly onto the gangplank, and then bolted for cover.

I made it as far as the sewage tank, where I huddled in the shadow and tried to catch my breath. My heart was beating so hard that I thought my chest might split open. Behind me I could hear Dusty's goon cussing and kicking at the spilled poker chips. When I looked back, I saw him moving through the gambling boat and shining a flashlight.

It seemed like a fine time to run away.

But as I rose to my feet, a car came bouncing down the dirt road toward Dusty's dock – a police car, with its headlights off. Immediately I dove back to my hiding spot, which would have been a nifty move except that I banged my head on the sewage tank.

The pain was ridiculous. At first everything went bright, like a starburst, and then suddenly it was as black as a tunnel. My skull was ringing like a gong.

As I lay there, trying not to cry out and give myself away, I heard my own voice say out loud: *It's empty. Empty!*

It wasn't my skull that was ringing; it was the sewer tank.

Which should have been full, if the *Coral Queen* had emptied her hose into it that night.

I watched the police car roll to a stop near the boat. The bald goon hurried down the gangplank and waved at the deputy, who hopped out of the car and followed Dusty's man onto the boat. Both of them were shining flashlights back and forth.

I rolled to my knees and sat up too fast. As I waited for the dizziness to go away, I noticed a dark, powdery tracing on the concrete slab under the sewage tank – something so small that the pollution inspectors might never have noticed. I touched it and, in the faint light from the docks, saw red on my fingers.

Rust. The old tank was rusting away.

I reached underneath and found a patch of pitted metal that crumbled like stale crackers. Peeling it away, I made a hole so large that I could stick my fist inside.

The sewer tank wasn't just empty, it was wrecked and useless – a phoney prop in Dusty Muleman's scam.

Suddenly the knot on my head didn't hurt so much. I stuffed a handful of rust into my pocket, and took off.

EIGHT

The next afternoon Mom insisted on driving all the way to Homestead for groceries because nobody there knew who she was. Dad's TV interview was the buzz of the Keys, and she didn't want to deal with the stares and whispers at the local market.

After she and Abbey left, I sat down and watched the tape. My father was in rare form. He looked straight into the camera and declared: 'I sunk the *Coral Queen* as an act of civil disobedience.' He said he was protesting the destruction of the oceans and rivers by 'ruthless greedheads'.

The jailhouse jumpsuit didn't look half bad on television, I had to admit. Dad had also combed his hair and put on his wire-rimmed glasses, so he came off more like a college professor than a boat vandal. This time he had the good sense not to compare himself to Nelson Mandela (or if he did, the TV people were nice enough to cut that part out). My father ended the interview by saying he intended to stay locked behind bars until the law dealt squarely with Dusty Muleman.

Next to show up on camera was a rodent-faced man who identified himself as Dusty's attorney. In a righteous tone he described his client as an experienced boat captain, respected businessman, and 'pillar of the community'. He said that Dusty would never purposely contaminate the waters where his own son played. The lawyer concluded by calling my father a 'mentally unbalanced individual', and challenged him to prove his 'reckless and slanderous allegations'.

As I was rewinding the tape, somebody knocked on the front door. It was Mr Shine, Dad's lawyer. For once he didn't look like he was on his way to a funeral.

'Hello there, Noah,' he said.

'Mom's not here.'

'Oh. I should've called first, but I just received some important news.'

'About Dad? What is it?'

Mr Shine sucked air through his teeth. 'Sorry. I'm obliged to tell your mother first.'

'Is it *bad* news?' I asked.

'No, I should think not.'

'Then tell me. Please?'

'I wish I could,' Mr Shine said.

Thanks a bunch, I thought. Couldn't he even give me a hint?

'Did you see him on TV last night?' I asked.

Mr Shine nodded with a sickly expression. 'I strongly advised your father against doing that interview.'

'But he's right, you know – about Dusty Muleman flushing the holding tank into the basin. Everything Dad said was true.'

'I'm sure he thought so at the time.'

'It's all going to come out sooner or later. You just wait.'

Mr Shine plainly didn't believe me. 'Please tell your mother that I'll call later,' he said, and turned to leave.

'Can I ask one more question?'

'Of course, Noah.'

'Is my mom going to divorce my dad?'

Mr Shine looked like he'd swallowed a bad clam. 'What?' he croaked. 'Where in the world did you get that idea?'

'Well, is she?'

He licked nervously at his lips. 'Noah, quite frankly, I'm not comfortable with this conversation.'

'Hey, *I'm* not comfortable with the idea of Mom and Dad splitting up,' I said, 'but Abbey and I have a right to know. Don't we?'

By now Mr Shine was backing away from the door. 'You should speak directly with your parents about these concerns,' he said, 'and in the meantime, don't jump to conclusions . . .'

For an older guy he could move pretty fast. In a matter of moments he had hustled to his car and sped away.

I went back inside and replayed the videotape of Dad's interview. I kept wondering what Mr Shine had come to tell my mother, although I had a feeling that his definition of good news might be different from mine.

Later I climbed up on the roof to readjust the TV dish, or try. I wiggled the darn thing around so that it was aimed upward at the sky, although I had no idea exactly where the satellites were orbiting. It wouldn't have surprised me to start getting MTV from Kyrgyzstan.

I unhooked the incriminating bucktail jig from the dish and started scaling down the rain gutter. Just then I heard honking, and a green Jeep Cherokee wheeled into our driveway. Shelly poked her blonde head out the window and hollered my name.

I dropped to the ground and went to see what she wanted.

'Hop in,' she told me, 'and hurry it up. I'm not gettin' any younger.'

I got in because I was scared to say no. The thought of Shelly chasing me down and dragging me feet-first into her Jeep was not appealing.

As I fumbled to put on the seat belt, she peeled

out of the driveway and raced toward Highway One. It was a while before I got up the nerve to ask where we were going.

'Why? You got a hot date or somethin'?' she said.

I decided not to mention the silver-barrelled gun that lay on the console between us.

'Shelly, is something wrong?'

She laughed sourly. 'You don't miss a trick, do you?'

Even though she was wearing black sunglasses, I could tell she'd been crying. She was still sniffling and her voice sounded scratchy.

''Member what I told you about Lice runnin' away?'

'Yes, ma'am.'

'Well, turns out I had it wrong,' she said.

'Did he come home?' I asked.

Shelly shook her head. 'They finally towed the Jeep back from Cutler Ridge. Two hundred bucks – I had to pawn my promise ring to pay for it,' she said. 'Know how I spent my morning, Noah?'

'No, ma'am.'

'Scrubbing bloodstains off the upholstery!'

I had thought it felt damp on the seat. 'Blood? You sure?'

'See, I missed a spot.' Shelly pointed to a dark reddish smudge on the dashboard. 'I don't think Lice ran

away,' she confided. 'I think he got snatched. And' –
here she made a hard left turn, nearly spilling the gun
onto my lap – 'I think whoever snatched him killed
him.'

'What!'

'That's right, Noah.' She buried her nose in a tissue.
'And I think it's all 'cause of your daddy and that
gamblin' boat.'

I'd never been so close to a woman with a tattoo –
or, I should say, a tattoo I could see for myself. Rado
claimed that his older sister had gone off to college
and gotten a tiny zebra butterfly tattooed on her butt.
Thom and I had to take his word for this, since neither of us had ever seen enough of Rado's sister to
confirm the story.

Strange as it sounds, the more I stared at the tattoo
on Shelly's arm, the more natural it looked. The barbed
wire definitely suited her personality.

'Relax. The pistol ain't real,' she said. 'It's a lighter.'

When she pulled the trigger, a bright blue flame
flared from the barrel.

'It looks pretty bad, though, huh? Bad enough to
scare anybody tries to give me trouble,' Shelly said.

For more than hour we'd been heading down the
highway, obviously to nowhere in particular. Shelly
kept saying she had more to tell me, but then she'd

get worked up about Lice Peeking and what a 'total zero' he was, and how she must be a fool to care about him. Afterward she'd cry and sniffle for a while, but just when I thought she had a grip on herself it would start all over again.

We were all the way to Sugarloaf Key before she turned the Jeep around and grumbled, 'Where the heck was I goin'?' On the way back she pulled into the parking lot on the Marathon end of the old Seven Mile Bridge. The place was full of tourists who were tinkering with their cameras, getting ready to shoot pictures of the sunset. It was too cloudy for a green flash, and besides, I was too distracted to stand there and look for it.

'What makes you think Lice is . . . you know . . .'

'Dead? Number one, he hasn't called up beggin' to come home,' Shelly said, 'which is totally not like him. Number two, none of his local party pals have heard from him, not a peep. Number three was that ugly bald gorilla who came to the trailer that night, and number four was the blood in my car.'

Again she pointed at the stain on the dashboard. I tried not to stare at it. Shelly being so worried made me worried, too.

'But who would kill him? And what's it got to do with my dad?' I asked.

She sighed impatiently. 'Noah, you got any idea

how much money Dusty Muleman makes off the *Coral Queen?*'

'No, ma'am.'

'Between fifteen and twenty grand just from the casino tables,' she said. 'Subtract the food for the customers, the pay for the crew, and he's still clearin' ten thousand, minimum, every night.'

'*Dollars?*' I couldn't believe it.

'Gambling is a mega-huge business, kid, because the world is crawlin' with suckers,' Shelly said. 'Don't forget that Lice had a big mouth. Suppose he blabbed to somebody that he was gonna help your daddy, and suppose Dusty found out. He'd have a cow if he thought the feds were gonna rush in and shut down the *Coral Queen.* How far do you figure he'd go to stop that from happenin'? You're a smart boy, Noah, think about it.'

I didn't want to think about it. I didn't want to believe that Dusty Muleman had murdered Lice Peeking, all because my father had made a deal with Lice to get his testimony.

She said, 'Don't worry, I'm still gonna keep my promise. I'm gonna help you clear your daddy's name.'

'But why?'

'Maybe 'cause it's the right thing to do. Or maybe 'cause now I've got a dog in this fight.'

'You want to nail Dusty, too.'

'If he hurt my man, you bet I do,' Shelly said. 'If he harmed one hair on that lazy, worthless, lice-covered head . . .'

She was either tougher than I'd thought, or crazier than I'd thought.

'It's way too dangerous,' I told her. 'Forget about it.'

'Too late.'

She stuck the gun-shaped cigarette lighter in the waist of her jeans and got out of the Jeep. She was still limping slightly from kicking the toilet bowl, but apparently her foot wasn't broken. I followed her onto the old bridge, where we leaned against the warped railing and looked down at the green-blue water ripping through the pilings. The sun was halfway gone, and all around us the cameras were clicking.

'What else did you want to tell me?' I asked Shelly.

'This morning I went to see Dusty.'

'Alone? That's nuts!'

'Noah, I used to live with the man. We were engaged to be married, for God's sake,' she said. 'Anyhow, I asked could I have back my old bartending job on the *Coral Queen*. I gave a big sob story about Lice bailin' out on me, and how I was hurtin' for money.'

The breeze delivered a whiff of Shelly's tangerine perfume, which actually smelled pretty nice. I noticed she was wearing only two silver hoops in each ear, and I figured that maybe she'd pawned all the others, like her promise ring.

'Did Dusty give you the job?' I asked.

'Yup. I start tomorrow night.'

Shelly had guts, no doubt about it. She was going undercover to nail Dusty Muleman, the man she suspected of ordering her boyfriend killed. It was odd, but she looked more sad than scared.

I said, 'Please don't do this. Stay away from that boat.'

'What if I told you I really *did* need the dough.'

'It's not worth it,' I heard myself say. 'I don't want something bad happening to you, too.'

'Aw, nothing's gonna happen.' Now she sounded like the old Shelly, incredibly calm and sure of herself.

'If you're not afraid, how come you're carrying around that fake gun?' I asked.

'Good question.' She took the lighter out of her jeans and casually tossed it off the bridge. 'I was gonna start smokin' again, but you just talked me out of it. Thanks, Noah.'

She smiled, and then did something totally outrageous. She leaned over and kissed the top of my head, the way Mom used to do when I was small. It was just a quick peck, but I felt my face turn red.

'My momma used to say, "Keep your friends close,

girl, but keep your enemies closer,"' said Shelly. 'Don't worry about me, Noah. I know how to handle Captain Muleman.'

A few of the tourists started clapping, which they sometimes do in the Keys at the moment the sun disappears over the horizon. Why, I've got no earthly idea. Sunset on the water ought to be a quiet and easy time, but I guess some people can't stand a little silence.

'Speaking of mommas,' Shelly said, 'yours'll start freakin' out, we don't get you home pretty soon.'

That night, before bed, I took the rust dust out of my pocket and showed it to Abbey. I told her all about the bogus sewage tank at thc boat dock; about Lice suddenly disappearing and the bloodstains in the Jeep; about Shelly going back to her old job on the *Coral Queen* to help us nail Dusty Muleman.

Abbey was her usual sceptical self. 'You're saying that the same goon who grabbed me at the marina kidnapped Lice Peeking and snuffed him? No way.'

'It's a possibility,' I said.

'In Miami, yeah. But this is the Keys!'

When I told her how much money Dusty was making from the casino boat, Abbey's eyes widened.

'What if we went to the police and told them everything?' she asked excitedly.

'They'd think we're a couple of whack jobs. We need witnesses, Abbey, not just a hole in a sewer tank.'

'Does this Shelly person have a plan?'

'We're still working on it,' I said.

'*We?* Oh, great.'

'Any ideas would be welcome.'

'Noah, this isn't a game,' my sister said. 'If there's a killer out there – which I doubt, but if it's true – there's only one possible plan.'

'Which is?'

'We pack up and move to Canada immediately. You, me, Mom, Dad – we drive straight to Saskatchewan and move in with Grandpa Kenneth and Grandma Janet. Why are you looking at me like that?'

'Good night, Abbey.'

I was so tired that I fell asleep in my clothes. Right away I started dreaming about fishing, which wasn't unusual for me. In the dream I was alone in a small wooden boat, hooked up to a humungous tarpon that was dragging me out to sea. The water was getting rougher, and the salt spray was whipping at my cheeks and stinging my eyes. Before long it got dark and I couldn't see a thing.

All I had to do to save myself was let go of the stupid fishing rod, but it was the biggest tarpon I'd ever seen and I wanted desperately to catch it. The fish was pulling so hard that the little boat was ploughing and lurching through the waves. Somehow I managed to steady myself in the bow, leaning with all my might against the muscle of the fish. Every so often the line would hiss upward, slacken, and then a tremendous splash could be heard in the distance. I knew it was the sound of my tarpon jumping, trying to shake out the hook.

Eventually the black gloom was broken by a bright white burst, and I realized we were passing the lighthouse at Alligator Reef. In the dream I started thinking about all the monster barracudas and sharks that lived on the reef, and what a bad thing it would be to tumble overboard there.

Next, something terrifying happened. The boat was lifted by an enormous claw-shaped wave and tossed like a toy, high in the air. The spinning rod flew from my grip and I pitched backward, expecting at any moment to crack my skull against the planks of the transom.

But instead I just kept falling, as if tumbling through a high mountain canyon. I tried to wake myself but I couldn't, which is the worst feeling when you're in the middle of a bad dream. As I fell, something invisible began rocking me back and forth – lightly at first, but then harder and harder until I was flopping around like a rag doll.

With both arms I swiped out blindly, groping for something to cling to. What I ended up grabbing was a round, mossy-topped rock – or so I thought, until the rock started speaking.

'Noah,' it whispered. 'Please let go of my face.'

I opened my eyes. 'Dad?'

'Sorry if I scared you.'

I bolted upright and reached for the lamp. There was my father kneeling by the bed, still wearing the orange jailhouse jumpsuit. He was definitely not part of my dream.

'It's good to see you, buddy.'

'Good to see you, too,' I said. 'But what are you doing here?'

'I escaped,' he replied matter-of-factly.

'Escaped? From jail?'

'I'm afraid they left me no choice.'

I didn't bother to ask who he was talking about because it didn't matter. This time he'd gone too far.

'Does Mom know you're out?'

'Not yet. I wanted to wake you and Abbey first.'

Sure, I thought, because he wanted protection. Mom wouldn't throw any heavy objects at him if we kids were in the room.

'It looks bad, I know,' he admitted, 'but I can explain.'

I doubted that seriously.

'Here's an idea,' I said. 'How about you try out your story on me, before we go see Mom?'

Dad grinned in relief. 'I knew I could count on you, Noah.'

NINE

Breakfast was surprisingly civilized, all things considered.

Dad had slept on the floor of my room, then surprised Mom first thing in the morning. She cried some at first, and they hugged for a long time. Abbey and I slipped out of the kitchen and parked ourselves in front of the television, which still wasn't working.

The TV-dish repair guy showed up while my mother was making eggs and pancakes, and he was still banging around on the roof when we all sat down to eat. I didn't volunteer any information about the broken satellite dish, and Mom didn't ask. Her attention was fixed on my father.

At first there was lots of easy talk and even a few laughs. He asked Abbey about her piano lessons. He asked me for a fishing report. He asked Mom if the washing machine was still leaking, and if Grandpa Kenneth had gone ahead with his double-hernia operation.

Finally, Dad set down his fork and said, 'Look, I

want to apologize for all the grief I've caused. I'm not sorry I sunk the *Coral Queen*, but I admit that my judgement was clouded by frustration and impulsiveness and . . . well, anger.'

So what else is new, I thought.

'Have you ever heard of a gag order?' he said.

Abbey glanced at me irritably. I looked at my mother, who was obviously waiting for Dad to explain why escaping from jail was such a grand idea. At her request he'd taken off the orange jumpsuit and put on a pair of jeans with a T-shirt. To a visitor he would have appeared completely normal.

'The sheriff got a lot of flak from Dusty Muleman and his buddies after I went on Channel Ten,' Dad was saying, 'so he decided I couldn't do any more interviews. Basically he gagged me! Not literally, but you know what I mean. Meanwhile Channel Seven is calling, the *Miami Herald*, even NPR! That's National Public Radio!'

'We know what NPR is,' Abbey said thinly.

'Go on, Paine,' said my mother, her voice tight.

'Honestly, I didn't know what to do. None of the deputies at the jail were talking to me any more,' Dad said. 'So I just sat alone in my cell, reflecting on the fact that this country was founded on the bedrock of free speech. It was colonized by people who'd been forbidden to express themselves in their homeland,

and were determined to build a new society that was open and free.'

'Unless you happened to be a slave,' I pointed out.

'A valid point, Noah. The settlers who came to America weren't saints, that's true,' said my father, 'but the principles they put into law were solid and just. And here I was, rotting in jail, deprived of my freedom to speak out by some small-minded, small-town bureaucrat with a badge. It was just wrong, so wrong.'

Dad wasn't acting. He truly believed that even a jailbird has a constitutional right to go on television.

'Last night, after they brought me dinner – if you could call it that – there was a bad car accident on the highway in front of the sheriff's station. Some drunk rolled his convertible. All the deputies ran outside to help.'

'So you just waltzed out the back door,' Abbey said.

'They forgot to lock my cell!' Dad looked to me for moral support. 'It was one of those moments that called for a split-second decision.'

'You could've decided to relax and eat your dinner,' I suggested.

'But how could I stay there, muzzled like a dog?' my father said. 'What good could I possibly do, stuck in that situation? People need to be told what's going on around here. They need the truth!'

He paused, as if waiting for someone to applaud. We didn't.

'So I hid for a couple of hours in the woods behind the hardware store,' he went on quietly, 'and then I made my way home.'

Abbey picked at her pancakes. I poured myself another glass of orange juice. We'd heard his whole story the night before. Now it was time for Mom to weigh in.

She said, 'Paine, there's something you ought to know. Mr Shine got some interesting news yesterday about the *Coral Queen* case.'

'Like what – Dusty confessed?' Dad said dryly.

'No, but he agreed to drop all the charges. He promised not to prosecute if you promise to stop spreading stories about him. He also wants you to get some psychological counselling,' my mother said.

'That's good news? He wants me to play like I'm crazy?'

'It shouldn't be hard,' Mom said tersely. 'Whatever it takes, I want you home. And so did the sheriff, by the way. He called yesterday to tell me they were bringing two prisoners up from Big Pine for a court hearing and they needed both jail cells. He'd planned to release you this morning, bail or no bail. He's already lined up a judge to sign the order.'

'Meaning . . .'

'Aw, don't tell me.' Abbey slapped a hand to her forehead.

'That's right,' my mother said. 'Paine, you didn't need to escape. They were getting ready to evict you.'

Dad slumped in his chair. I looked over at him and gave a sympathetic shrug. 'Bad timing,' I said.

'But are they allowed to do that?' he asked miserably. 'Can they kick a person out of jail, even if he refuses to put up bail? I don't think so.'

Mom said, 'In this county they can. Trust me.'

For several moments we all stared at our cold eggs and pancakes and thought about the absurdity of the situation. Eventually my father said, 'Oh well. It all turned out the same anyhow. No harm done.'

'Wrong,' Mom said crossly. 'The judge hadn't signed your release papers yet, so technically you did commit a jailbreak. That's a felony, Paine – worse than sinking Dusty's casino boat! This time they could send you to a real prison.'

Dad folded his arms thoughtfully. 'So I *am* a fugitive after all.'

'Congratulations,' Abbey muttered.

My mother was thoroughly exasperated. '*No harm done?* Are you kidding me?' she said to my father.

'Donna, all I meant was—'

He was spared by a knock on the door – the TV-dish repair man, waiting to be paid. Mom wrote him a cheque and returned briskly to the table.

'Paine, here's what we're going to do now,' she said, plucking the phone off its cradle. 'We're going to call Mr Shine and tell him to arrange for you to turn yourself in. Then, if the sheriff is in a generous and forgiving mood, he'll go ahead and release you – legally, quietly, and without further embarrassment.'

The word 'embarrassment' hung in the air like a foul smell. Still, Dad didn't seem to comprehend how much trouble he was in with Mom.

He said, 'Honey, I'm not sure I can turn myself in to these people. There are principles at stake, basic human rights.'

My mother turned to me and Abbey. 'Could I speak to your father alone, please?'

Outside, a car door slammed. Dad stiffened up.

My mother put down the phone. 'Noah, see who that is.'

Abbey was already at the window. 'It's a cop,' she reported anxiously.

'No!' my father blurted, and hightailed out the back door.

Mom was so calm that it was spooky. She picked up Dad's plate and placed it in the sink. When the deputy rang our doorbell, she told us to stay in the kitchen while she went to talk with him.

Abbey and I quickly cleared the rest of the table and started washing the dishes. We were so nervous that we worked like robots – she scrubbed, I dried and stacked.

The deputy didn't stay long, which was a relief. I'd figured he would tear the house apart searching for Dad, but he never even stepped inside.

When Mom walked back into the kitchen, she smiled in a sad and tired-looking way. She was carrying some folded clothes, a toothbrush, and the paperback chess book that I'd brought to Dad in jail.

'The officer was simply returning your father's belongings,' Mom said. 'Apparently the sheriff is delighted that he escaped and has no intention of pursuing him – as long as he goes back and gets the paperwork straightened out.'

'You want me to look for him?' I asked.

'I'd appreciate that,' Mom said. 'Abbey, could you run outside and water my orchids?'

My sister eyed her. 'You're trying to get rid of me. How come?'

'Because I need to speak with Noah privately.'

'The orchids died last January,' Abbey said with a smirk, 'during the freeze. Remember?'

'Then go water the roses,' said my mother.

*

I found him at Thunder Beach. He was barefoot and hatless, sitting in the sunshine by the water.

'This is the place where you learned to swim,' he said.

I sat down in the sand beside him.

'Abbey, too,' he added. 'Your mom and I used to bring you here almost every weekend. By the time you were three, you could dive to the bottom all by yourself and pick up a conch shell. You remember?'

'Not really, Dad. I was too little.'

'Know how this place got its name? A man was killed here in nineteen forty-seven by a bolt of lightning. Bright clear day, not a cloud in the sky. All of a sudden – ba-boom! The thunderclap was so loud, it busted the windshield out of a dredge at Whale Harbour.'

'Who was he?' I asked.

'The man who died? I believe he was one of the Russells or maybe an Albury, I'm not sure. But he was standing right about here on the beach, cleaning his cast net, when it happened. He'd caught about three dozen mullet, and they all got fried to a crisp by that lightning bolt,' my father said. 'Your Grandpa Bobby told me that story a long time ago. Why they call it Thunder Beach.'

I couldn't help but notice how unusually sunny and clear it was. Dad must have seen me squirming because he said 'Don't worry, son, it was a freak deal – what they call an atmospheric anomaly. Probably never happen here again in million years.'

'Dad, come on home.'

'But what if it's a trap? The sheriff, setting me up.'

'It's not a trap. The sheriff never wants to lay eyes on you again,' I said.

The water boiled and a barracuda broke the surface, slashing through a school of needlefish.

'I'm right about Dusty dumping crap in the water,' Dad said.

'I know you are.' I told him that the sewage tank at the dock was broken, and how the crew of the *Coral Queen* had faked hooking up the hose to it.

'I figured it was something like that,' he said bitterly. 'Lice Peeking knows all about that scam, I bet.'

'Dad, I've got more bad news. Lice Peeking is gone.'

'No!'

I told him about the bald guy with the crooked nose coming to Lice's trailer, and about the bloodstains Shelly found later in her Jeep.

'She thinks Dusty Muleman killed Lice, or had him killed, to shut him up,' I said.

My father looked horrified. 'I can't believe that,' he said, but his voice was shaky.

'Abbey thinks we should pack up and run to Canada,' I said.

'What do *you* think, Noah?'

'I think it's awful cold up there.'

'No doubt,' he said quietly.

'And those snowmobiles, Dad, they're even noisier than jet-skis.'

'That's a fact.'

'So we'll figure something out. We always do,' I said. 'Come on home.'

Dad was lost in thought, staring gloomily up the shoreline toward the mouth of the basin where the *Coral Queen* was moored.

He said, 'Dusty offered to drop the charges against me because he doesn't want the bad publicity from a trial. And he got rid of Lice as a warning to anyone else who knows the real story about the casino boat, anyone who could back me up.'

'Makes sense,' I said.

'But if Lice is really dead, it's all my fault.'

'No, Dad. If Lice is dead it's because he was greedy,' I said. 'He didn't want to tell the truth unless he got money for it. If he'd gone to the coast guard way back when, like he should have, Dusty would've been shut down a long time ago. So let's go home. Please?'

'The water looks clean today, doesn't it? Though you can't always tell just by looking.' He got up and slowly waded in, trailing his fingers along the surface.

'Your Grandpa Bobby used to bring me down to

the Keys three, four times a year,' he said. 'When I was about your age, I stood right here and watched him catch a fourteen-pound muttonfish off the wings of a stingray.'

'On what?' I asked.

'A chunk of frozen shrimp,' Dad recalled. 'I bet there hasn't been a mutton snapper on these flats in ages. Lots of reasons – fish trappers, pollution, too many boats. That's what people do when they find a special place that's wild and full of life, they trample it to death.'

He spun around to face me. 'Noah, you under-stand why I sunk the *Coral Queen*, right? Every time Dusty empties her holding tank, it's like flushing a hundred filthy toilets into God's ocean!'

It made me sick to think about it. Still, I couldn't afford to let my father get himself all wound up again. There was something else I needed to tell him; some-thing even more important.

'Mom wants you to come home right now,' I said. 'She said it's not open for debate. No more speeches, she said, no more excuses. Just come home.'

'Aw, she'll settle down.'

It was like talking to a brick wall . . . so I took out the sledgehammer.

'Dad, listen to me,' I said. 'Mom's thinking about filing for divorce.'

'What? No way!'

'I overheard her say something on the phone to Grandma Janet.'

My father stood knee-deep in the water, blinking and cocking his head like he wasn't sure if he'd heard me right.

'She actually used that word. *Divorce?*'

'Loud and clear. She's already spoken to Mr Shine. Abbey was eavesdropping.'

'Oh man,' Dad sighed. 'What a mess.'

At long last, reality seemed to be sinking in. I could see he was really worried about what Mom might do next. So was I.

'Come on,' I said, 'let's go.'

He reached down and scooped up a baby blue crab, which he cupped in his hands. When he bent down to inspect it, the crab promptly fastened its miniature claws to his nose and hung there, like a weird painted ornament. My father and I broke out laughing until the crab let go and plopped back into the water.

'Go tell your mom I'll be home shortly,' he said. 'We'll take the skiff out this evening – you, me, and Abbey. Catch some snappers for supper.'

I felt pretty good when I hopped on my bike and headed for home. I'd done the tough job that I needed to do, and Dad had responded the way I'd hoped. As I rode along, my thoughts were still bouncing all over the place and I wasn't paying attention to what was ahead of me.

Unfortunately.

One second I was pedalling full speed, the next I was hurtling over my handlebars. I landed hard on my right shoulder and rolled. When I came to a stop, I was flat on my back.

Staring up at the pinched, angry face of Jasper Muleman Jr.

'Hey, dorkbrain, where's your training wheels?' he said.

I heard a dumb hick laugh that was unmistakably Bull's. He and Jasper Jr must have spotted me coming and ducked into the woods to wait. I sat up and saw my bike on the ground, a freshly snapped gumbo limbo branch sticking out of the front spokes.

'That's original,' I said to Jasper Jr.

Bull snatched me up by the collar and dragged me into the trees. I could hear Jasper Jr running after us. When we got to a clearing, Bull straightened me up, spun me around, and pinned my arms.

Jasper Jr got right in my face. 'So where's your big white-trash bodyguard? The one who knocked over my wheelbarrow.'

I wondered if he already knew that something bad had happened to Lice Peeking.

'He wasn't my bodyguard,' I replied. 'He was my personal chauffeur.'

Jasper Jr said I was a real comedian. Then he hauled off and slugged me in the gut.

'That's for Snake Creek,' he snarled, 'for making me sink my johnboat.'

The punch knocked the wind out of me, and I went limp as a noodle in Bull's grip. I remember thinking of something clever to say, but all I could do was squeak like a leaking balloon. It seemed to take for ever to catch my breath, and right away Jasper Jr slugged me again.

'And that's for your crazy father sinking my father's boat,' he said.

At that point the world turned fuzzy and grey, and I thought I was history. My mouth was flapping but absolutely nothing was coming out.

I heard Jasper Jr say, 'Bull, you wanna turn?'

'No, bro, I'm good,' Bull said, and let me drop to the ground.

Immediately I closed my eyes and let my tongue hang out and pretended I was dead. It might work fabulously for possums, but it sure didn't work for me.

Jasper Jr kicked me so hard in the thigh bone that his big toe made a sharp popping sound. He started hopping around and hollering that I'd busted his foot.

Bull remarked that it was usually a smart idea to put on shoes before you started kicking somebody. Jasper Jr told him to shut up and gimped away, moaning. I heard Bull chuckling as he followed his wounded friend back to the road.

I would've been chuckling, too, if it hadn't hurt so much.

TEN

It isn't easy pretending everything's wonderful when you feel like you've been thrown off the roof of a building. Luckily, there weren't any bruises that Mom or Dad could see because this time Jasper Jr had socked me in the stomach (not my eye), and the ugly knot on my thigh bone was covered up by my pants.

I didn't tell my parents what happened because they would've freaked and gone straight to Dusty Muleman, or maybe even the police, which was not how I wanted to handle it. So I just sat around like a lump in front of the television, trying not to move. In the summer I'm always outdoors – fishing or snorkelling or skateboarding – so Abbey got suspicious about me hanging around the house every day. Mom thought it was weird, too, but she was busy keeping an eye on my father.

Mr Shine had arranged for Dad to return to the jail and surrender himself. The sheriff couldn't wait to send him back home, although a judge put him under 'house arrest' until the *Coral Queen* case was settled. To keep track of his whereabouts, they clipped an electronic bracelet on Dad's right ankle. If he stepped so much as three inches past our front door, a signal would beep at the sheriff's station and they'd come after him again.

For a week we were like a semi-normal family, except that my father wasn't allowed out of the house. One of us always stayed with him, not just to keep him company but also to make sure he didn't try anything cute, like prying off the ankle bracelet.

We played lots of video games and watched fishing shows on ESPN and didn't talk at all about Dusty's casino boat. Abbey's new project was building an Olympic village for hermit crabs, and Dad really got into it. Abbey and I collected the crabs (there were scads of them in the woods along the Old Highway) while my father sat at the kitchen table working with his tools. Before long he'd put together a miniature track, a lap pool, a pole vault, even a hurdle run.

Unfortunately, the average hermit crab isn't particularly athletic, having to haul a clunky seashell around on its back, so the sports competition part of Abbey's project sort of fizzled. Most of the crabs hunkered down and refused to budge. Still, it gave Dad something to do that kept his mind off the *Coral Queen*.

Until Shelly showed up late one afternoon.

Abbey watched her get out of the Jeep and said, 'This oughta be good.'

Shelly was dressed in her casino-boat bartender's outfit, which was loud and skimpy. She wore high heels and stockings that looked like they were made from a mullet net. As I opened the door to let her in, I decided it was probably a good thing that Mom wasn't home.

'Long time no see,' Shelly said to my father, and gave him a brisk, businesslike hug. Then she introduced herself to Abbey, who was gawking at the barbed-wire tattoo on Shelly's bare arm.

'How about something cold to drink?' Dad offered.

'Iced tea would be super. I can't stay long,' Shelly said.

We all sat down in the living room, Shelly crossing her legs and sipping her tea. My father was on the edge of his seat, looking like he was dying to pepper her with questions.

'How you doin', Noah?' Shelly said to me.

'Great.'

'Feelin' OK?' She gave me a narrow look to let me know that she knew I wasn't telling the truth. It was creepy how sharp her radar was.

'So, how's work?' I said, eager to change the subject.

'Work is work,' Shelly replied. Then, turning to

Dad: 'Paine, what's that thing on your leg?'

My father explained about the electronic bracelet. 'I'm on house arrest. You believe it?'

'Boy, that really sucks,' Shelly said.

Out of nowhere Abbey asked about the tattoo. That's one thing about my sister, she's not afraid to say anything.

Shelly smiled and traced one finger along the dark blue links. 'That's a story for when you're older,' she said. 'It was a long night and a bad party.'

'But why barb wire?' Abbey always called it 'barb' wire.

'To show the world how rough and tough I was,' said Shelly. 'To be honest, I wish it was daisies instead. This thing's gonna look mighty stupid when I'm eighty years old and my grandkids are askin' how come I got a cow fence painted on my arm. Hey, Paine, can you take a bath with that ankle gizmo, or would you get all electrocuted?'

Dad laughed. 'Naw, it's waterproof.'

'Amazing,' Shelly said.

'Any word from Lice?' I asked hopefully.

She shook her head. 'But I got some other news. That's why I stopped over.'

We waited as she glugged a long drink from her glass.

'They're at it again,' she said. 'Dumpin' the toilet

tanks into the water. Last night I stayed late to restock the bar, and I saw it for myself. Dusty was already gone with the money, and I guess the crew didn't know I was still there.'

I noticed that my father's fists were clenched on the arms of his chair. Abbey saw it, too.

'They just hung the hose off the side of the boat,' Shelly went on, 'like it was business as usual.'

'What time was this?' Dad asked.

'Between one and one-thirty. The marina was empty,' Shelly said.

Abbey spoke up again. 'That man is major scum.'

'No doubt,' said Shelly. 'And here's what else. The big bald guy with the Z-shaped nose? The one who came to see Lice that night before he went missing? His name's Luno, and he's Dusty's main muscle. I think he's from Morocco or someplace like that.'

I purposely didn't look at Abbey. Neither of us had told my father that she'd bitten Dusty's goon that night at the marina when he snuck up and grabbed her. Dad would've gone bonkers if he found out.

And Mom, well, forget about it. We'd already be halfway to Saskatchewan by now.

'What if they get suspicious and start hassling you?' I asked Shelly.

'Why would they? Think about it from Dusty's point of view. Why would I come back to work for him if I knew he and Luno were mixed up in Lice's death? Heck, I'd have to be suicidal, right?' Shelly winked. 'Naw, Dusty bought the whole sad story. He thinks I wanted my job back just because Lice left me broke. And I'll be honest, the money's not too shabby.'

Dad stood up and started pacing back and forth.

'Well, I'd better be off,' Shelly said.

'How are things going with Dusty?' I asked.

'Oh, don't worry about that. He's under control.'

'You be careful,' my father told her.

'Yeah, well, don't go sinkin' that boat again,' Shelly said, 'especially if I'm on it.'

Then she said goodbye and breezed out the door, leaving us in silence with a light sweet scent of tangerines.

That night Abbey barely touched her dinner. She said she didn't feel well and asked to go to bed early.

Mom tucked her in and returned to the table. 'I think your sister's got a touch of the flu. Are you feeling all right?'

'Fine,' I said.

'Paine?'

'Never better,' said my father.

'Did you call the taxi company?' Mom asked.

'Tomorrow. I promise,' Dad said. He was supposed to make sure that they were holding his job for him.

'Actually, I was thinking of trying to get my captain's licence back,' he said matter-of-factly, 'so I could guide in the backcountry again.'

My mother put down her fork. 'You can't be serious.'

'Well, why not?'

'After what you did to the casino boat, you honestly believe the coast guard will let you take customers back out on the water?' she said. 'Honey, you'll be lucky to get your cab back.'

Dad stabbed at a green bean and let the subject drop.

'Somebody from the *Herald* phoned while you were in the shower,' Mom said. 'I explained that you won't be giving any more interviews. Right?'

'Yeah,' my father mumbled. One of the conditions for Dusty Muleman dropping the criminal charges was that Dad stop ranting to the press.

'You know, he's started flushing his holding tanks again,' Dad said. 'It's true. Ask Noah.'

Mom looked at me, then back at my father. 'How do you know this?'

'We've got our sources,' Dad said mysteriously.

'Someone who works on the *Coral Queen*,' I added.

'I see,' my mother said. 'Then this "source" of yours should go straight to the authorities and make a report. That's the way it's supposed to be done. Noah, please pass the rice.'

'But Dusty's got connections with the coast guard and the cops,' Dad complained. 'They won't do diddly unless somebody catches him red-handed.'

'And maybe somebody will,' said Mom, 'but whoever that "somebody" is, they don't live in *this* house. I've made my last visit to the jailhouse, is that understood?'

That night I couldn't sleep, so I dug out a stack of old skateboarding magazines. It was real late, well past midnight, when Mom peeked into my room and saw that I was still awake. She sat down on the bed and told me she was sorry that dinner had gotten a little tense. Everything would get back to normal, she said, once Dad's legal problems were over and he was working again.

It took every ounce of courage, but I had to ask: 'Did you mean what you said to Grandma Janet about a divorce?'

Mom took a short breath and pressed her lips together. 'You heard me on the phone that night? I'm so sorry, Noah – I was extremely upset . . .'

I could tell she wanted to give me one of those big smothering hugs, like she used to do when I was small. This time, though, all she did was reach over and touch my hand.

'Your father is a very unusual and intense personality,' she said, 'as I'm sure you've noticed. I love him dearly, but sometimes he drives me bananas. More than sometimes, truthfully.'

'I know, Mom.'

'Look, I understand that he gets terribly upset by certain things he sees in this world – greed and injustice and cruelty to nature. That's one of the things that first attracted me, seeing how deeply he cared. But he's a grown man,' my mother said, 'and he needs to start behaving like one. I don't care to be married to a jailbird.'

'So you *were* serious,' I said.

'I'd never bluff about something like divorce. It wouldn't be fair to you and Abbey.'

I didn't need to tell Mom how worried we both were. She knew.

'Speaking of your sister,' she said, 'I'd better peek in and see how she's feeling.'

I said good night and turned out the light and pulled the covers up to my neck. I heard Mom open Abbey's door and say her name. Abbey didn't answer, so I figured she was already asleep.

But then Mom started calling out for my father in a voice that didn't even sound like hers, it was so choked up. Dad came running down the hall from one direction, and I came running from the other.

When we entered Abbey's room, my mother was standing there with tears in her eyes. Her knuckles were pale and pressed to her cheeks, and her shoulders trembled.

'She's gone!' Mom cried. 'Abbey's gone!'

My sister's bed was empty. The window was wide open, and the screen, which had been removed, was propped against the bedroom wall.

'OK, everybody take it easy,' Dad urged. I could tell he was trying to calm himself, as much as me and my mother.

He tried to wrap his arms around Mom but she jerked away. 'Somebody kidnapped her, Paine! Somebody broke in and took her!'

'No, Mom, nobody took her,' I said.

'How do you know? How?'

What could I say? Sometimes I sneak out my bedroom window late at night to go bridge fishing or crabbing with Thom and Rado. One time I got back and Abbey was hiding in my room, watching me as I climbed in through the window and put back the screen. She never ratted me out to my parents, but obviously she'd remembered the trick.

'A kidnapper wouldn't bother to stack the screen against the wall,' I pointed out. 'He'd just cut his way through with a knife.'

'Noah's absolutely right,' Dad said. 'This is way too neat and tidy. It's pure Abbey.'

Mom wiped her eyes on my father's sleeve. 'So

what you're saying is, she ran away? Why in the world would she do that?'

'I don't think Abbey ran away,' I said.

'Noah, get to the point.'

'She probably just had something she needed to do.'

'In the middle of the night? All by herself?' My mother turned to my father and froze him with one of her deadly laser-beam stares. 'Paine, what's going on here?'

'I'll be right back,' Dad said, and rushed out of the room.

Mom spun back toward me and snatched me by the left ear.

'Young man?' she said.

She never called me 'young man' unless she meant business.

'Yes, Mom?' I was almost sure that I knew where Abbey had gone. And I had a feeling that Dad had figured it out, too.

'Does this have something to do with the *Coral Queen*?' my mother asked.

'It's possible,' I said weakly.

'Has this whole family gone completely insane?' She let go of my ear and called out: 'Paine! You come back here right this second!'

Moments later Dad appeared at the bedroom

door. He had put on a ball cap, a pair of khaki trousers, and his old deck shoes. In one hand was the portable spotlight that he kept stowed on the skiff.

'Where do you think *you're* going?' Mom demanded.

'The video camera is missing,' my father said.

'Answer my question. Where are you going?'

'To find Abbey,' Dad replied evenly.

'Paine, you're under house arrest. Remember?'

My father sheepishly pulled up the right leg of his pants to reveal a bare ankle.

'Oh, that's just terrific,' said my mother. She was not normally a sarcastic person, but she could be brutal when she was. 'I'll go pack your suitcase for state prison,' she said to Dad. 'Will they let you bring your own pyjamas?'

'Donna, please. There's no time to argue.'

'Oh, really? Our little girl is roaming around alone in the dead of night, and meanwhile you've tripped off some fugitive alarm at the sheriff's station, and any minute a dozen squad cars with screaming sirens will be racing down our street—'

'I'll go get Abbey by myself,' I volunteered. 'Don't worry, Mom, I can handle it.'

'No, we'll go together. All three of us,' she declared. 'And if we get into a jam, I want both of you wise

guys to keep your lips zipped and let me do the talking. Is that understood?'

My father and I glanced helplessly at each other. There was no point in objecting.

'Noah, get a can of bug spray out of the pantry,' Mom said. 'And, Paine, could you please go find my car keys?'

ELEVEN

Mom drove, both hands on the wheel. She stuck to the speed limit because she didn't want the police to pull us over and find my father in the car.

When she turned down the road to the marina, Dad leaned out the passenger window and began shining the spotlight through the mangroves, in case Abbey was hiding there. He lit up a family of raccoons and a grouchy blue heron but there was no sign of my sister.

We were more than a hundred yards from the docks when Mom stopped the car. I suggested that we split up and start searching, but Dad said no way, it was too risky. We got out of the car and together headed toward the boats.

Every so often my mother would call out Abbey's name while Dad probed the shadows with the spotlight. As we approached the marina, I could see that the *Coral Queen* was dark, though a light shone in the ticket shack at the foot of the dock. I put a finger to my lips, signalling for my parents to stay quiet.

Parked by one of the lampposts was Dusty Muleman's long black SUV.

We huddled in the shadow of the broken sewage tank. Dad had snatched a rusty gaff from a dock box near one of the charter boats, and I could tell by the sound of his breathing that he was agitated and pumped up. Mom, however, remained calm.

Dad said, 'You two stay here. I'll go scope it out.'

'You'll do no such thing,' my mother told him. 'Tonight we're a team.'

Dad started to argue, but then he stopped and cocked his head to listen. I heard it, too – a man's laughter, coming from inside the ticket office.

'What if he's got Abbey?' I whispered anxiously.

'Then we'll politely ask him to give her back,' Mom said. 'And if that doesn't work, we'll try something else. Come on.'

My mother only weighs 110 pounds, but she doesn't think small. She walked up to the shack and rapped on the door and didn't wait for it to be opened – she just barged in Dad and I were right behind her.

'Why, look who's here!' said Dusty Muleman, hanging up the phone.

He was sitting under a bare light bulb at a wobbly card table. Piled in front of him were stacks of cash and tally sheets from the gambling boat.

Mom said, 'Dusty, I apologize for the interruption but this is very important.'

'No problem, Donna.' He looked highly amused by the sight of us.

'Have you seen Abbey tonight?' my mother asked.

'Abbey? What would she be doing hangin' around this place?' Dusty scoffed.

Dad started edging forward with the tarpon gaff, which wasn't good.

'She went looking for pilchards,' I piped up. Sometimes the boat basins were loaded with little fish, which Dusty Muleman knew for a fact. 'We're supposed to go fishing tomorrow and she decided to catch her own bait.'

Dusty didn't fall for my story. 'Abbey ain't much bigger'n a pilchard herself. I'd sure like to see how she throws a net,' he said. 'What's she doing out so late, anyway? Most little girls would've been tucked in beddy-bye a long time ago.'

'Have you seen her?' Mom asked again. 'We're getting worried.'

'Nope.' Dusty was wearing a baggy, fruit-coloured shirt that was decorated with palm trees. A fat soggy cigar wagged in the corner of his downturned mouth. Fortunately it wasn't lit, otherwise we would have gagged on the smoke in that closet-sized room.

'Let me check with Luno,' he said, and spoke gruffly

into a walkie-talkie. Then he looked up and addressed
my father: 'Paine, I'm a little surprised to see you out
and about. The sheriff told me you were under house
arrest.'

'I was,' Dad said, 'until my daughter went missing.'

His jaw was set and his shoulders were bunched.
He was wound up as tight as a spring, and I thought
that any second he might pounce on Dusty Muleman,
who was smaller and flabbier.

Mom must have been thinking the same thing. She
snatched the sharp gaff from my father's hand and
carefully placed it upright in a corner.

'Dusty, listen,' she said. 'Paine's got something he
wants to say.'

'I do?' Dad said.

'Yes, you do. Remember?' my mother replied point-
edly. 'You wanted to apologize for what happened to
the *Coral Queen*.'

I burst out coughing like I was having a seizure. I
couldn't help it.

'Apologize?' my father said numbly.

'Yes, Paine, we had this discussion the other night.'
Mom's tone was pleasant but determined. 'You and
Dusty have known each other too long to let this kind
of situation get out of control.'

'Donna's right,' Dusty said. 'All those years we
fished out of Ted's, we never had a problem.'

Dad was steaming, but there wasn't much he could do. Dusty had promised to drop the criminal charges only if Dad agreed to behave. Mom must have figured that this was as good a time as any for Dad to start acting remorseful, even if he didn't mean it.

'Fine,' my father said stiffly. 'I'm sorry for sinking your boat.'

'Apology accepted.' Dusty smacked on the cigar, and his shifty grey eyes swung to me. 'Son, I heard from Jasper Jr that you've been givin' him a hard time.'

'You're kidding, right?' I said.

Dusty shook his head. Dad looked at me curiously.

'No, it's the other way around,' I started to protest. 'He and Bull . . .'

'He and Bull *what*?' asked Dad.

'Nothing.'

'Noah, what's going on?' my mother said, like she'd already forgotten about my black eye. I figured she just didn't want to stir up more trouble, with Abbey missing and Dad's future freedom in Dusty Muleman's hands.

Still, I had to bite back the urge to tell everything that had really happened between me and Jasper Jr. Dusty was clearly enjoying himself at my expense. He knew the truth, too. I could see by the way he smirked.

'I know it's gettin' more and more like Miami

down here,' he said, 'but a boy still ought to be able to go fishin' without having to fight his way home. Don't you folks agree?'

'Absolutely,' said my mother, although this time I detected a slight chill in her voice. When she glanced at me, I knew that she didn't believe a word Dusty Muleman was saying.

I also understood that she expected me to suck up my pride and do what was best for the family, as my father had done.

'Tell Jasper Jr it won't happen again,' I said to Dusty.

'That's the spirit.' He gave me a gloating wink.

The door swung open and Luno appeared. Up close the man was even taller and uglier than I remembered. His slick bald dome glowed pink in the pale light, and his smile was as crooked as his nose. A swatch of dirty-looking gauze was taped on one of his branch-sized forearms, probably where my sister had chomped him. In one hand he carried a walkie-talkie like Dusty's; in the other hand was a half-empty bottle of beer.

'What's up, chief?' he said to Dusty.

'You seen a young girl hanging around the docks tonight?'

'Girl?'

'Little kid,' Dusty said. 'Curly brown hair, if I remember right.'

'Ash blonde,' corrected my mother.

Luno's shark eyes flicked to the wound on his arm. I wondered if he'd ever admitted to Dusty that he'd been bitten by a pint-sized trespasser. I also wondered if Luno recognized me as the one who'd slugged him that night on the charter boat.

If he did, he didn't let on. His gaze revealed nothing but icy and casual indifference, and I had no doubt he was capable of anything – even killing Lice Peeking.

Dad didn't seem even slightly intimidated by the bald-headed goon, which is one of my father's problems. Sometimes he doesn't know when to be afraid.

'No girl here tonight,' Luno said with a shrug.

'We want to look around for ourselves,' Dad declared.

Dusty said, 'Luno says she's not here, she's not here. You can take it to the bank.'

'Please,' said Mom. 'We won't be long.'

'Suit yourself. I got nothin' to hide.' Dusty took the cigar out of his mouth. 'So, Paine, I meant to ask you – how're the anger management classes goin'?'

Part of the deal for Dusty dropping the charges was that my father would sign up for 'professional counselling'. Dad thought it was ridiculous, of course.

My mother said, 'We've got an appointment with a therapist in Key Largo, as soon as Paine gets off house arrest.'

Flush

'Outstanding!' said Dusty.

'Yeah, I can hardly wait,' Dad mumbled.

'Listen, man, you can't go around sinkin' other people's boats just because you get some wacko idea in your head,' Dusty told him. 'You need to get a grip. Seriously.'

'He will,' Mom said.

My father's face reddened.

'Let's go look for Abbey,' I said.

Luno went along, probably to make sure that we didn't go snooping anywhere Dusty didn't want us to go. We traipsed from one side of the basin to the other, up and down the charter docks. Dad and Mom kept shouting my sister's name, but the only response was some crazed dog barking its head off – a big old German shepherd that one of the captains kept chained on his boat.

When we returned to the ticket shack, the light was off and Dusty had gone. Luno leaned against the fender of his beat-up station wagon and folded his beefy arms.

'See? Girl no here,' he said. 'You go away now.'

Mom and I turned to leave, but Dad didn't move. He stood there nose to nose with Dusty's goon. It was too dark to make out their expressions, but the tension in the air was like the hot static buzz you feel before that first clap of thunder.

'If anything's happened to my little girl,' Dad warned in a low voice, 'I'll be back for you and your boss man.'

Luno grunted out a harsh chuckle and rasped something in a foreign language. Whatever he said, it didn't sound like he was the least bit worried by my father's threat.

Mom spoke up. 'Paine, let's go.'

Being a sensible person, she was nervous in Luno's presence.

'Paine, please,' she said again. 'It's late.'

Slowly Dad pivoted his shoulders and began walking away. Feeling the heat of Luno's glare, the three of us trudged down the dirt road. Mom and I kept swatting at mosquitoes that were buzzing around my father, who hadn't bothered to use the bug spray. He didn't seem to notice the annoying little blood-suckers, or maybe he didn't care.

Once we were safely inside the car, my mother took a deep breath and said, 'All right, Noah, where should we look for your sister now?'

Unfortunately, I didn't have a Plan B. I'd been so sure she'd gone to spy on the *Coral Queen* that I hadn't even considered any other possibilities.

'Let's just drive,' Dad said glumly, fiddling with the switch on his spotlight.

In the glow from the dashboard his face appeared

to be covered with odd black freckles – but then I realized that the freckles were actually more mosquitoes, too gorged with blood to fly away.

'Maybe Abbey went home already,' I said hopefully. 'She's probably already back in bed, sleeping like a log.'

Mom nodded. 'Yes, that's where we should go next. She'll worry if she sees my car is gone.'

'And what if she's not there? What then?' Dad asked.

'Then we call the police, Paine,' my mother said with a hitch of anger.

There wasn't much to discuss after that. Mom drove slowly up the dirt road, away from the marina. Dad couldn't get the spotlight working, so he started cussing and pounding on it with the heel of his hand. Finally he just gave up and flipped on the radio.

My mother had to make a wide turn onto the Old Highway, to avoid hitting a possum. She stepped on the gas and rolled down the windows to blow out the bugs.

Dad was sunk down in the passenger seat, his head bowed. Mom was humming some old Beatles song, trying to act as if she wasn't all that worried, but I knew better. She was doing fifty-two in a thirty-mile-per-hour zone, which for her was some kind of speed record.

We had gone maybe a mile or two when I spotted a flash of something in the distance along the side of the road, something larger than the usual Keys critters.

'Mom, slow down!' I said.

'What?'

My father looked up. 'Donna, stop!' he exclaimed.

'Oh, for heaven's sake,' Mom said, and hit the brakes.

Together we broke out laughing, all three of us, in pure relief.

There, in the headlights, stood my little sister. She was wearing her backpack, her white Nikes with the orange reflectors on the heels, and, hanging from a shoulder strap, our video camera. Her skinny bare legs glistened with insect repellent.

As always, Abbey was well prepared.

She grinned and stuck out a thumb.

'How about a ride?' she called out.

TWELVE

My parents were so thrilled to find Abbey that they couldn't even pretend to be mad about her sneaking out the bedroom window. They made us go to bed as soon as we got home, but she was up early the next morning, insisting on showing the videotape that she'd made at the marina.

I was impressed by what my sister had tried to do, but she's no Steven Spielberg. The tape was so dim and shaky that it was almost impossible to see what was going on.

Abbey was bummed. She scooted closer to the TV and pointed at the fuzzy image. 'There's the hose! See, they're dropping it right in the water!'

Dad asked, 'Honey, where were you hiding – up a telephone pole?'

'Tuna tower,' my sister said over her shoulder.

It was a cool idea, actually. A tuna tower is the tall aluminium platform that sits above the cockpit on a deep-sea charter boat. The captain climbs to the top so he can spot game fish crashing bait from far away. It would have been a perfect roost for secretly filming the casino boat, except for a couple of problems.

First, Dad's video camera wasn't one of the newer models, so the picture was lousy when it was dark outside. Second, my sister never quite figured out how to zoom the lens, so everything on the tape was extremely small and grainy. You could make out the profile of the *Coral Queen*, but the crew looked like June bugs crawling around the deck.

'It's not your fault,' Mom told Abbey, 'it's the camera's.'

'But I can still see what they're doing – can't you?' My sister stabbed her finger at the TV. 'That's the hose from the holding tank right . . . *there*.'

'Now I see it,' I said.

'Me too,' said my father.

We really weren't sure what we were looking at, but we didn't want to hurt Abbey's feelings. She popped the cassette out of the camera and announced, 'All we've got to do is take this to the coast guard, and Dusty Muleman is toast!'

Mom and Dad exchanged doubtful glances. Neither wanted to be the one to tell Abbey that her videotape was useless.

'I know what you're thinking,' said my sister, 'but they've got supercool ways to enlarge the image and make it crystal clear. The FBI and CIA do it all the time – they can count the zits on a terrorist's nose from a mile off!'

A car door slammed in the driveway, startling us. We don't get much company at seven in the morning.

Mom looked out the window and said, 'Paine, it's a deputy.'

'Oh, not again,' Abbey groaned.

'Try to stall him,' said my father. 'Noah, come with me. I'll need your help.'

We hurried down the hall to my parents' room, Dad locking the door behind us. The electronic bracelet was hidden beneath the bed, along with the tools he had used to remove it. I held the heavy plastic collar around his right ankle while he worked feverishly with needle-nose pliers, a screwdriver, and a hex wrench.

'Hold extra still,' he whispered. 'One little slip and I could break the transmitter.'

From the living room we heard the low tone of the deputy's voice, politely saying, 'No, thanks. Really, I'm fine.' It sounded like Mom and Abbey were trying to feed him breakfast.

Moments later I heard my mother's footsteps, followed by a light rap on the door. 'Paine, are you up yet? There's a gentleman from the sheriff's department here to see you.'

'Be out in a minute,' Dad drawled, trying to sound sleepy.

From the intense way he was gripping the tools, I knew my father truly didn't want to go back to jail – but that's where he was headed if we didn't get the bracelet clamped back on his ankle.

'Almost there,' he murmured, pausing to wipe the palms of his hands. Both of us were sweating, we were so nervous.

There were more footsteps in the hall, only this time they were too heavy to be my mother's. This time the knock on the door was sharp and impatient.

'Mr Underwood? Open up, please, this is Deputy Blair from the sheriff's office. Mr Underwood?'

Another hard knock.

I motioned for Dad to hurry. He looked up, smiled, and made an 'OK' sign with his fingers.

When I let go of the bracelet, it held fast to my father's leg. The police would never know it had been unfastened for a night, or so we thought.

Now the doorknob began to jiggle. On impulse I grabbed up the tools and rolled under the bed.

My father opened the door. 'Sorry to keep you waiting, Officer, but I was putting on some clothes.'

'Step this way, sir,' I heard the deputy say, in a tone that wasn't particularly friendly.

*

My dad was an awesome fishing guide. Everybody in the Keys said so. Tarpon, bonefish, redfish, snook – Dad was dialled in on all of them. He could put his customers into fish when the other guides were getting skunked. My mother said it was a special talent he inherited from Grandpa Bobby.

We all knew how much Dad missed being out on the boat every day. He never complained, but he was basically miserable driving a taxi up and down the highway. Three different times he'd gotten rear-ended by other cars while crossing one of the bridges. That's because he always slowed down to stare out at the open water. He couldn't help himself – scoping out the tides, the depth, the wind direction, all the things that were important if you were hunting fish.

After the third accident, my father's boss at the cab company got on his case. Dad pointed out that, technically, none of the rear-enders had been his fault. It had always been the other drivers who'd gotten the tickets, for following too close.

But his boss didn't care. It was costing him money every time the cab was off the road, in the body shop. 'One more crash,' he'd warned my dad, 'and you're fired.' The guy acting like he was Donald Trump.

I had a hunch he wouldn't hold Dad's job open after what happened with the gambling boat, and I was right. When Mom called the taxi company, the owner told her that he'd hired a new driver the day my father got arrested. Mom told us that she didn't blame the guy – he had a business to run. Still, I knew she was worried. The bills were piling up, and her paycheque wasn't nearly enough to cover them all.

It would be a while longer before Dad could start searching for a new job, because now he was back in jail.

I don't know if Dusty Muleman ratted him out, or if the electronic ankle bracelet was programmed to send a certain signal when somebody messed with the lock. In any case, the sheriff ordered my father hauled in again, for 'tampering with a court-ordered monitoring device'.

He wasn't in a great mood when I went to visit.

'This is really getting old,' he said wearily. 'You didn't have to come today, Noah. This place is the pits.'

In a way I was glad to find my father depressed, because that was a perfectly normal reaction to being in jail – and Dad acting normal wasn't something you could take for granted. He was a much different person from the happy camper I'd visited there only three weeks ago.

'I bet your mother's really ticked off,' he said.

'What for?' I said.

How could any of us be mad at him? The only reason he'd pried off the stupid ankle monitor was so that he could leave the house to hunt for Abbey. Any father would have done the same thing if one of their kids had disappeared in the middle of the night.

'Mom's trying to get hold of Mr Shine,' I said.

'Tell her not to bother. They're only keeping me for forty-eight hours,' Dad said, 'to, quote, teach me a lesson. Talk about a waste of tax dollars!'

'What should we do with Abbey's video?' I asked.

Dad shook his head. 'God bless her, she really tried. But you saw the tape, Noah. If we took it to the coast guard, they'd laugh.'

He was probably right. 'So what now?' I asked, and mentally tried to brace for whatever new scheme my father had dreamed up.

He cut a dark glance toward the broad jowly deputy, who was leaning against the door. The man was thumbing through a motorcycle magazine, but I assumed he was listening to every word we said.

'It's over, Noah,' my father said with a sigh. 'I'm done with Dusty and the *Coral Queen*. I just want to come home and live a quiet, semi-normal life.'

'Really?'

'Really.'

I searched his face for some familiar hint of mischief, but it wasn't there.

'I know when I'm beat. I know when the ball game's over,' Dad said.

If he was putting on an act for our babysitter-deputy, it was a good one. He looked totally tired and fed up, and his voice rang flat with defeat.

'Abbey's little adventure was the last straw,' he said. 'She risked her neck just to prove I was right about the casino boat. But you know what, Noah? Being right isn't worth squat if you're endangering the people you love. If anything bad had happened to your sister last night, I'd never forgive myself. Never.'

I shuddered to think what that creepy Luno might have done if he'd caught Abbey sneaking around with the video camera.

Dad leaned forward and lowered his voice. 'Look, I wasn't trying to be some kind of hero when I pulled the plugs on Dusty's boat. I was only trying to stop him from using the ocean as a cesspool. And it back-fired, OK? So now—'

'Time's up.' The deputy slapped shut his magazine.

My father squeezed my arm. 'Things'll be different when I get home. That's a promise, Noah.'

I left the jail with mixed-up feelings. I wanted things to be different at home, for Mom's sake, but I sure didn't want Dad to make himself into a whole different person.

Yet maybe there was no other way.

*

Later Abbey and I packed a lunch and rode our bikes to Thunder Beach. It was one of those bright hazy days with no horizon, when the sea and the sky melt together in a pale blue infinity. The heat rippling off the dead-calm water made the lighthouse seem to flutter and shimmy in the distance.

We sat down on the warm sand and ate our sandwiches and shared a bottle of water. I tried to gently tell Abbey the truth about her videotape, but she was one step ahead of me – as usual.

'It stunk, I know,' she said. 'I already erased it.'

'You had a cool plan. It's not your fault it didn't work out.'

'Yeah, whatever.'

When I told her what Dad had said at the jail, she got quiet for a while. Finally, she said, 'So that's a good thing, right? Him promising to behave.'

'I guess. Sure.'

A cherry-red speedboat went tearing past the beach, then made a tight circle and roared back in our direction. The driver was a muscle-bound guy with so much gold hanging from his neck, it was a miracle he could sit up straight. He slowed to an idle and shouted something to a large blonde woman who was sunning herself alone, about fifty yards from Abbey and me. The speedboat's engine was so loud that we couldn't hear what the man said, but the woman got up and sweetly motioned him to come closer to shore. When he did, she beaned him with a beer can.

'Whoa, baby!' Abbey exclaimed. 'She could play quarterback for the Dolphins!'

'I think I know who that is,' I said.

The speedboat took off at full throttle, the driver heaving the beer can over the side. When he rooster-tailed past us, he was scowling and rubbing his fore-head.

'You know that lady? Oh, don't tell me.' Abbey peered curiously at the blonde sunbather. We were too far away to be able to see the barbed-wire tattoo, or the hoops in her ears.

'Follow me,' I told my sister.

Shelly was shaking the sand off her towel when we walked up. She was wearing a neon-yellow swimsuit and round mirrored sunglasses. Her face was smeared with so much zinc oxide that it looked like she'd fallen nose first into a frosted cake.

'Well, if it isn't the amazing young Underwoods,' she said.

'What did that guy in the red boat say to you?' Abbey asked with her usual bluntness.

'He asked me for a date, sort of,' said Shelly. 'But he needs to work on his manners.'

'You sure nailed him good,' I remarked.

'Trust me, he deserved it.' She winked at Abbey.

'Now if he was Brad Pitt and not some loser gym monkey from Lauderdale, it's a whole different story. I'd be sitting beside him right now, speeding off to Bimini.'

I told Shelly that Dad was back in jail.

'That really bites,' she said. 'You guys want somethin' to drink?'

Abbey took a Coke, but I said no thanks. I noticed the beer can that Shelly had used to clobber the speedboat driver was floating about twenty yards off the beach.

She frowned. 'Man, I hate litterbugs.'

'Me too,' I said, and started wading out.

'Hey, stud, where do you think you're going?'

'To get the beer can. It's no big deal,' I said.

'It is too a big deal,' said Shelly. 'Check out the water, Noah.'

I glanced down and felt my stomach pitch. The shallows had a darkish yellow tint. Strands and clots of foul, muddy-looking matter floated here and there, around my legs.

'What is it?' Abbey asked.

'Something seriously gross,' I said. Now I could smell it, too.

'Then get out!' Abbey shouted.

'That'd be my advice, too,' said Shelly. 'And pronto.'

As disgusting as it was to be wading through the

Coral Queen's toilet crud, I couldn't leave that beer can out there to float away.

Whenever my father takes us out on the boat, he always stops to scoop up trash that other people have tossed overboard – Styrofoam cups, bottles, chum boxes, plastic bags, whatever. Dad says it's our duty to clean up after the brainless morons. He says the smart humans owe it to every other living creature not to let the dumb humans wreck the whole planet.

So what we Underwoods do is pick up litter wherever we see it.

Even when it's drifting in sewage.

When I came sloshing with the beer can out of the shallows, Abbey stepped back and said, 'Noah, that is *so* nasty!'

'I guess it's true,' Shelly said, 'that the nutcase doesn't fall far from the tree.'

'What does that mean?' I asked.

'It means you're just like your old man. Here, gimme that thing.' With two fingers Shelly plucked the can from my hand and held it at arm's length, like it was radioactive.

'Notice the dent,' she observed with a chuckle. 'Gym Monkey must've had a hard noggin.'

She dropped the can into a tall trash barrel. Then she turned back to me. 'I told you Dusty was dumping again, didn't I?'

It wasn't like I'd forgotten. From where Abbey and I had been sitting earlier on the beach, the water had looked normal and safe. Once you stepped in, though, it was a different story.

Shelly said, 'OK, Nature Boy, now you run straight home and scrub yourself down in a hot shower.'

'Don't worry.' I was already busy scraping at my leg with a sea-grape leaf.

Abbey stood at the water's edge, gazing out in heavy silence. Shelly put an arm around her tense little shoulders and said, 'Let's hit the road, kiddo. Before your flaky brother gets any more bright ideas.'

Abbey turned to me. 'The fish are gone. Those little green minnows we always see here.'

'They'll be back,' I said, 'when the water clears up.'

Suddenly a loggerhead stuck up its knobby brown head. It might have been the same one that I'd seen that day with Thom and Rado, but I couldn't be sure. One turtle head looks a lot like another.

'No!' my sister cried out. 'Noah, do something!'

The loggerhead obviously didn't know it was swimming in filth. I began jumping and clapping my hands together, trying to spook it away from the beach, but that didn't work. The turtle floated lazily at the surface, blinking up at the sun.

Abbey began to shake and cry. Shelly told her not

to worry, turtles were tough customers. 'They've been on this old planet a lot longer than we have. They're survivors,' she said.

'Not this one,' my sister sobbed. 'Not if she gets sick from the bad water.'

Abbey was right. Absolutely right.

So I charged back into the waves, kicking and splashing and hollering like a lunatic. It wasn't the brightest thing I've ever done, but it definitely got that loggerhead's attention. In a fright it ducked under and scooted off, leaving only a boiling swirl.

This time nobody said much when I came out of the dirty water. Abbey looked like she wanted to give me a hug, but she was understandably reluctant to get slimed. Shelly just shook her head in disbelief and tossed me a towel.

Together we trudged down the beach to a paved lot where her Jeep was parked. 'Promise me you'll go home and wash up,' she said.

'Promise,' I said.

'And, Abbey, promise me that you'll try to keep your brother from getting into more trouble.'

'You bet,' Abbey said half-heartedly.

Shelly looked around to make sure the three of us were alone, which seemed obvious since her Jeep was the only car in the lot.

'I'm going to tell you guys somethin', but you don't

know where you heard it, OK?' She leaned close, and the air turned to pure tangerine. 'There's a man who works at the coast guard station, a civilian named Billy Babcock. He's got a major gamblin' problem, you understand? He's addicted to it.'

'You mean like drugs,' Abbey said.

'Yeah. Or booze,' said Shelly. 'Billy can't stop betting no matter how hard he tries. Blackjack, dice, roulette, you name it. He's a regular on the *Coral Queen,* like, four nights a week. Sometimes more. You see where this is heading?'

I did. 'Does he owe Dusty money?'

Shelly nodded. 'Big time. So much money that Billy couldn't pay it all back if he lives to be a hundred.'

'So he's repaying it another way.'

'You got it, Noah,' Shelly said. 'Every time the coast guard gets ready to pull a surprise inspection on the *Coral Queen,* Billy Babcock calls Dusty the day before to warn him. That's why they never catch 'em emptying the tank.'

Abbey flopped her arms in dismay. 'So Dad was right after all. Dusty *is* being tipped off.'

'Hey, you didn't hear it from me,' Shelly said.

'But—'

'Shhhh!' Shelly pointed toward a white pickup that was rolling into the lot.

The truck pulled up and parked near the Jeep.

Stamped on the door of the cab was: DEPARTMENT OF PARKS AND RECREATION.

A man in a tan uniform got out and gave us a friendly nod. From the bed of the pickup he removed a small sledgehammer, a half dozen metal posts, and a stack of cardboard signs.

'You folks on your way to the beach?' he asked.

'What's up?' said Shelly.

The man showed us one of the signs. DANGER, it warned in big letters. BEWARE OF CONTAMINATED WATER.

Beneath those words, in smaller red lettering, it said: SWIM AT YOUR OWN RISK.

'Contaminated with what?' asked my sister, acting as if she didn't know.

'Human waste,' said the man from Parks and Recreation. 'We got a call from a guy who was fishing out here this morning. The health department came and sampled the water – it tested off the charts. You all might want to try Long Key, or maybe Harris Park.'

'Sounds like a plan,' Shelly said, playing along.

After the man went off to post the warning signs, my sister and I said goodbye to Shelly and began walking to our bikes.

'Noah, what you did back there for that sea turtle, that was very . . .'

'Dumb? I know.'

'No. Cool,' Abbey said, 'in a really twisted way.'

'Thanks, I guess.'

'We can't give up on this,' she added grimly.

'Now you sound like Dad.'

'Well? *You're* the one who went into that scuzzy water – twice! Doesn't it make you furious?'

'Yeah, it does.'

Furious and sick at the same time. But I thought of Abbey's spying mission the night before, and what a disaster it could have been. I'd never forget the cold-blooded look in Luno's eyes when he saw us standing in Dusty's ticket shack.

'Mom doesn't need any more excitement from us,' I told my sister.

'She won't have to know a darn thing,' Abbey said, 'because next time we'll do it right.'

The 'we' was a given. I wasn't about to let my sister go anywhere near that marina again without me.

We unlocked our bikes and started pedalling home in the thick July heat. I knew I stank from the crappy water, but Abbey claimed she didn't smell a thing. I kept thinking about how easy it was for Dusty Muleman to get away with what he was doing. With so many big boats on the water, nobody had been able to trace the pollution along Thunder Beach directly to the *Coral Queen*.

Or maybe nobody had tried hard enough.

It was time that somebody did.

'We can't get Dad involved in this, either,' I said to Abbey. 'He's had enough trouble already.'

'Definitely.' She grinned. 'Noah, does this mean you've got a plan?'

'Don't get carried away,' I said, which ought to be the Underwood family motto.

THIRTEEN

Dad was serious about getting serious.

The same morning he was released from jail, he went out and got himself hired by a company called Tropical Rescue. It wasn't the sort of work that my father could put his heart into, but I knew why he took the job.

It was the boat.

They let him use a twenty-four-foot outboard with a T-top and twin 150s – not for fishing but for towing in tourists who ran out of gas or rammed their boats aground.

Normally my father has no patience for these sorts of bumblers. He calls them 'googans' or even worse, depending on what kind of fix they've gotten themselves into. But Dad needed the job, so he buttoned his lip and kept his opinions to himself.

Unless it's a life-or-death emergency, the coast guard refers disabled-boat calls to private contractors like Tropical Rescue, which charge big bucks. They stay busy, too. It's amazing how many people are too lazy to read a fuel gauge, a compass, or a marine chart. They just point their boats at the horizon and go. All around the Keys you can see their propeller trenches – long ugly gouges, like giant fingernail scrapes, across the tidal banks. It takes years for the sea grass to grow back.

Dad's first rescue job was a boatload of software salesmen from Orlando who were stranded all the way out at Ninemile Bank. Somehow they'd managed to beach a brand new Bayliner on a flat that was only four inches deep. That's not easy to do, unless you're bombed or wearing a blindfold.

Miraculously, Dad restrained himself from saying anything insulting. He didn't get mad. He didn't make fun of the bonehead who'd been driving the boat.

No, my father – the new and improved Paine Underwood – stayed calm and polite. He waited patiently for the tide to come up, tugged the Bayliner off the bank, and towed it back to Caloosa Cove. He told us he almost felt sorry for the software salesmen when he handed them the bill, which didn't even include the hefty fine from the park service for trashing the sea grass. It was probably one of the most expensive vacations those guys ever had.

Even though Dad didn't like dealing with googans, he was ten times happier on the water than he was driving a taxi. That meant Mom was in a better mood,

too, laughing and kidding around the way she used
to do.

The two of them were getting along so well that
Abbey and I were extra careful not to mention the
sticky subject of Dusty Muleman's casino boat. We
discussed our new plan of attack only when we were
alone and away from the house, where our parents
couldn't hear us.

A couple of days after my father got out of jail,
the Parks Department took down the pollution warnings at Thunder Beach. The next morning, Abbey and
I put on our bathing suits and grabbed a couple of
towels and dashed outside. Mom and Dad figured we
were heading for the park, which is exactly what we
wanted them to think.

Because we were really going to Shelly's trailer.

I had to knock a half dozen times. When she finally
came to the door, she didn't seem especially delighted
to see us. Her eyes were puffy and half closed, and it
looked like somebody had set off a firecracker in her
hair.

'Time izzit?' she asked hoarsely.

'Seven-thirty,' I said.

She winced. 'A.m.? You gotta be kiddin' me.'

Abbey said, 'It's important. Please?'

We followed Shelly inside. She sagged onto the sofa
and tucked her legs up under her tatty pink bathrobe.

'Killer headache,' she explained, running her tongue across her front teeth. 'Large party last night.'

She was clearly in pain, so we got straight to the point. 'We need your help,' I said, 'now.'

'To do what?'

'To stop Dusty Muleman. You promised, remember?'

She laughed – one of those tired, what-was-I-thinking laughs. She looked across at Abbey. 'And *you* promised to keep your big brother outta trouble.'

'We won't get in any trouble,' Abbey said evenly, 'if you help us.'

It sounded like Shelly was having second thoughts. I wondered if she really *was* afraid of Dusty Muleman after all.

In a discouraged voice she said, 'I don't know what we can do to stop him. He's tight with all the bigshots in town.'

'But he's poisoning Thunder Beach,' I said. 'You know how sick a kid could get from swimming in that bad water? Same goes for the fish and the dolphins and the baby turtles. It sucks, what Dusty is doing. It's awful.'

'Yeah, but—'

'And don't forget what happened to Lice,' I added. 'Remember how you told me you had a dog in this fight? Remember—'

'Lice is exactly what I been thinkin' about,' Shelly

cut in. 'Say they really killed him, OK? You s'pose they'd hesitate to do the same to me or you, if somethin' goes wrong?'

It was about time she got worried, and who could blame her? If she was right about Lice being dead, then Dusty and Luno were cold-blooded murderers.

But one glance and I knew Abbey wouldn't back off, no matter what the risks. Neither could I.

'Shelly, I know it's dangerous—'

'Not to mention crazy,' she said.

'Yeah, and probably crazy,' I agreed. 'Look, if you don't want to be a part of this, it's OK. I understand.'

She shut her eyes and rolled back her head. 'Uh-oh, here comes the guilt.' She pressed her knuckles to her ears. 'Enough already, Noah. This poor blonde head's about to explode.'

Shelly stretched out on the sofa. Abbey got some ice cubes from the refrigerator and wrapped them in a dish towel, which Shelly gingerly positioned across her brow.

After a minute or two of muffled moaning she said, 'Guess I wasn't feelin' so brave when I got up this mornin', but hey, a promise is a promise. Count me in.'

Abbey and I looked at each other with happy relief.

'So what's the big plan?' Shelly asked. 'And how does your daddy fit in?'

'He doesn't fit in. We're not telling him about it,' Abbey replied.

Shelly opened one bloodshot eye and studied us. 'That's probably a darn good idea,' she said.

'But he'll still get blamed for everything – if we get caught,' I pointed out. 'That's why we need you.'

Shelly sighed. 'So let's hear it.'

When we told her our plan, she didn't laugh or make fun. She just lay there, thinking.

'Well?' Abbey said impatiently.

Shelly levered herself upright, balancing the ice pack on her forehead. 'This idea of yours is so whacked,' she said, 'it just might work.'

'Does that mean you'll help us?'

'And all I gotta do is flush?' she asked. 'That's it?'

'That's all you've got to do,' I said. 'Flush, and flush often.'

The next thing that happened was all my fault. I wasn't paying attention.

Abbey and I were riding home slowly along the old highway, talking about the *Coral Queen*, when somebody rushed up on us from behind. Before I could wheel around, Jasper Muleman Jr grabbed my bike and Bull grabbed Abbey's, and together they dragged us backward into a stand of Australian pines.

Not again, I thought in a panic. It wasn't me I was frightened for – it was my sister.

No sooner had Jasper Jr knocked me to the ground than I heard Bull cut loose with a spine-chilling wail. Instantly I knew what had happened: he'd been too careless with Abbey.

'Make her let go!' Jasper Jr hollered at me.

'I can't.'

Jasper Jr jerked me to my feet. 'Underwood, you don't make her let go of Bull, I'll snap you like a twig.'

Bull kept on wailing. Abbey had sunk her teeth into his left earlobe and was hanging on like a starved alligator. Bull was at least a foot taller than her, so he had to be careful not to pull away or else he might lose the entire ear. Whenever he moved even a little bit, his wailing got louder. The boy was in serious pain.

'Make her stop!' Jasper Jr demanded. 'He's bleeding, man, can't you see?'

'Abbey, is Bull really bleeding?' I asked.

She nodded, causing Bull to crank up the volume. It was pitiful to hear.

Jasper Jr started throttling me by the shoulders. 'Make her quit, Underwood, make her stop!'

'One condition,' I said. 'You guys let her go free.'

Jasper Jr sneered his famous sneer. 'How 'bout this for a condition, dorkbrain? Your sister quits chewin' on Bull, else I start poundin' your head with a ripe coconut.'

Bull managed to calm himself long enough to offer his own opinion. 'The girl takes her teeth outta my ear, she walks. You got my promise, Underwood.'

'Hey, no way—' Jasper Jr began to protest.

'You shut up,' Bull snapped. He was looking at us with his thick neck bent toward the ground and his head positioned sideways, to give Abbey as much slack as possible. Considering the delicate situation, she seemed incredibly calm.

I didn't see a single drop of blood, but there was no reason to inform Bull that he wasn't really bleeding to death. 'So, guys, do we have a deal or not?' I asked.

'Deal,' Bull grunted.

'Yeah, whatever,' said Jasper Jr, spearing me with a bony elbow.

'All right then,' I said. 'Abbey, you can let go now.'

'Nhh-ugh,' she said through a mouthful of crinkled ear.

'Come on. Let go of Bull.'

'Nhh-ugh.'

'You want to catch some gross disease? He probably hasn't had a bath since Christmas,' I said.

Even *that* didn't make her quit. I knew why, too. She didn't want to leave me out there alone with the two of them.

'Honest, I'll be OK,' I said, which must have sounded incredibly lame. She knew I wasn't going to be. OK. She knew they were going to stomp me into hamburger meat.

'Nhh-ugh,' my sister said emphatically.

'Abbey, come on!'

There was no way I could let her stay there in the woods. Jasper Jr was a vicious punk who wouldn't think twice about beating up a girl half his size.

Bull said, 'I think I'm gonna hurl.'

Abbey chomped down harder, and the noise that came out of Bull didn't sound human.

Jasper jumped me again and put me in a headlock. 'Now listen, you little brat,' he snapped at my sister. 'We're gonna do this my way. I'll break your brother's neck, you don't spit out Bull's ear by the count of three.'

There was no response from Abbey, but now I saw true fear in her eyes. My face must have looked like a tomato about to explode, as hard as Jasper Jr was clinching down on me. I couldn't tell my sister what to do next because I couldn't squeak out a word.

'One,' said Jasper Jr.

Abbey hung on.

'Two . . .'

Abbey wasn't budging.

'Two!' Jasper Jr barked again.

I tried to wriggle free, but it was no use. Jasper Jr's forearm was locked tight against my throat, and it hurt to breathe. Everything in front of me started getting fuzzy and dark, and I figured I was about to pass out.

The next words I heard were: 'Try two and a half, shorty.'

The voice sounded too old and gravelly to be Jasper Jr, but I just assumed that my hearing was messed up because he'd squeezed all the oxygen out of my brain.

'Let him go!' the voice said again, and it clearly wasn't speaking to Abbey. It was speaking to Jasper Jr.

Who, to my complete surprise, immediately let me go. I fell to the ground and stayed on all fours until I caught my breath.

'You all right, Noah?'

I lifted my eyes in bewilderment. The voice belonged to a lanky, long-armed man with woolly, silvery hair. A gleaming gold coin hung from a tarnished chain around his neck. His craggy face looked like a mahogany stump, and on one tanned cheek was a scar in the shape of an M.

Anybody could see that the guy was old – and tough. Shirtless and barefoot, he leaned casually against the trunk of a tall pine. His weather-beaten cutoffs had been bleached grey by the sun, and a dirty red bandanna was knotted around his right wrist. The curly hair on his bare chest was as shiny as the hair on his head.

Jasper Jr wasn't the sharpest knife in the drawer, but he knew that the stranger meant business.

'We was only jokin' around,' he said timidly.

'That right?' The old pirate smiled in a way that caused Jasper Jr to go pale. Bull whimpered like a puppy but said nothing.

The stranger turned to my sister. 'Now it's your turn, Abbey. How 'bout you let loose of that boy?'

My sister's eyes got wide at the sound of her name. She released her grip on Bull's ear, stepped back, and began spitting vigorously into the bushes. Bull straightened up and pressed a fist to his throbbing ear, trying to stanch the invisible bleeding.

'Who are you?' I asked the old man. 'How'd you know our names?'

He brushed past me and went up to Jasper Jr, who looked like he desperately needed a bathroom.

'You ever bother these two kids again,' the old man warned him, 'and you'll dearly regret it. *Comprende?*'

Jasper Jr nodded shakily.

Bull was actually an inch or so taller than the pirate, but it didn't help him. The guy walked over and got square in his face. 'Pretty summer day, you can't think of anything better to do than hassle some helpless little girl? That's flat-out pathetic, son.'

'Helpless? She nearly took my ear!'

'I'd say you got off lucky,' the stranger said with a smile.

He winked at Abbey and me, and jerked a thumb over one shoulder. 'Y'all run on home. Hurry up, now.'

'Who are you?' my sister asked.

'Nobody. And that's the truth.'

He wasn't kidding around.

'Now get goin', both of you,' he said. 'Me and the boys are gonna finish our chat.'

Abbey and I quickly retrieved our bicycles and took off. As soon as we were out of the trees, we started pedalling for home as fast as we could.

'You ever seen that guy before?' Abbey asked breathlessly.

'I don't think so.'

'Then how'd he know who we were? Has he been spying on us or something? He looked kind of dangerous, Noah, you think he's dangerous?'

'Abbey, I honestly don't know.'

Maybe I should have been creeped out by the strange old pirate, but I wasn't. For some reason I believed everything he'd said in the woods.

Except the part about him being nobody.

*

It was an hour before dark when we got out to the islands called the Cowpens. They got the name because Indians supposedly kept sea cows penned up there a long time ago.

Dad tossed the anchor into a deep hole about two hundred yards from the main channel. The Tropical Rescue rowboat was much bigger than Dad's bonefish skiff, so there was plenty of room for Mom to ride along. She'd said yes, too, which was a nice surprise. She sat on the bow with her back to the sun and snapped pictures of us fishing.

Right away I got a couple of decent mangrove snappers, and Dad caught a fat keeper grouper. My sister reeled in a puffer fish that blew itself up into a spiny balloon – she said it looked just like her fourth-grade teacher.

Of course, Abbey and I didn't mention what had happened that afternoon on the way home from Shelly's trailer. Dad would have taken off after Jasper Jr, and Mom would have gone to the police to tell them about the strange old man.

Besides, my father liked things quiet and peaceful when he was out on the water. He didn't go for too much talking. He said it was disrespectful to nature.

After a while we put away our fishing rods and sat down to wait for the sunset. The sky to the west was mostly clear, except for a few wispy clouds and the long foamy contrail from a big military jet. Dad took a seat up front next to Mom, who handed the camera to Abbey. I dangled my legs off the starboard gunwale, where RESCUE was painted in bright orange lettering.

A flock of pelicans floated over us in the shape of a V and kept on flying, straight toward the great Gulf of Mexico. A light breeze was blowing from the southeast, rocking the boat just enough to make us a little drowsy. Abbey nudged me and cut her eyes toward our parents, who were actually holding hands.

Everything felt so good and so right, I had this feeling that we'd finally get to see the green flash. The evening was perfect for it.

Gradually the sun changed from gold to blazing pink and seemed to turn liquid as it dimpled the horizon. None of us said a word because we didn't want the moment to end.

People who've never seen a sunset at sea would be blown away. Time seems to slow down until finally that huge blazing ball looks like it's just hanging there, balanced on the far edge of the earth. In reality, though, it's dropping fast.

As the last rosy crescent melted into the Gulf, I felt myself leaning forward, squinting hopefully at the skyline.

Then the sun was gone, leaving a pale lemon

emptiness. I glanced over at Abbey, who was putting the camera away. She smiled and shrugged.

'Wow, that was gorgeous,' my mother whispered.

'Yeah,' said Abbey, 'but no green flash.'

'Maybe next time,' my father said, as he always did.

I turned my gaze back to the horizon and held it there, even as the rim of pink faded to darkness. I heard Dad hauling in the anchor and Mom zipping her windbreaker and Abbey asking if she could steer back to the dock, but still I couldn't take my eyes off the sky.

FOURTEEN

ifty-seven dollars and sixteen cents.

That's all Abbey and I could scrounge up – and fifty-one bucks of it was hers. I would've had more if I hadn't bought new skateboard trucks the first week of vacation.

'You think it's gonna buy enough?' Abbey asked on the way to the store.

'It'll have to,' I said.

I didn't know the exact size of the *Coral Queen*'s holding tank, but I guessed it carried a couple hundred gallons of waste. I also didn't know how much dye we could get for fifty-seven dollars and sixteen cents.

Abbey led me to the aisle where the food colouring was displayed.

'Blue won't work, right?'

'No, that wouldn't show up,' I agreed, scanning the shelves. 'What do they use this stuff for anyway?'

'Frosting. Desserts. All kinds of goodies.'

'Do they make an orange?'

'No, but here's fuchsia,' Abbey said.

'What?'

'That's how it's pronounced, Noah. *Few-sha*.'

I had no idea what fuchsia was, but it sounded like something you wouldn't want to step in.

'It's a hot reddish purple,' Abbey explained. 'Perfect for Operation Royal Flush.'

That was the code name for our secret mission to nail Dusty Muleman. We'd decided to use food-colouring gel instead of laundry dye because the gel wasn't made with chemicals that would harm the sea life. Even better, it was highly concentrated, which meant that a small amount would dye a lot of poopy water.

The plastic bottles were little, though, holding only an ounce. There was only one container of fuchsia on the shelf, so we asked a stock boy to go find more.

'How many you want?' he asked.

'Bring us all you've got,' I said.

When we got to the cash register, the checkout lady gave us the skunk eye as she tallied up the total.

'What in the world,' she said, arching an eyebrow, 'would you kids be doing with thirty-four bottles of food colouring?'

Abbey smiled sweetly. 'We're baking a birthday cake,' she said.

'Oh, is that right?'

'A very *big* birthday cake,' my sister added.

'And a very purple one, I see,' the checkout lady said, handing us the bag of bottles.

On the way home I kept looking behind us to see if we were being followed by the old pirate geezer. I couldn't stop wondering who he was, and how he knew us.

Abbey said he was probably a gnarly old mate from one of the sport-fishing boats, or maybe a bridge person who'd seen us around the island and overheard us calling each other by name.

Whoever he was, I kept my eyes peeled.

As we turned the corner of our street, someone called out to us. It was Bull, of all people, standing in front of the house. He waved as we rode up, though Abbey and I were too suspicious to wave back.

I hopped off my bike and asked, 'What's up?'

Bull seemed edgy and uncomfortable. I could see Abbey's teeth marks on his left ear, which was still puffy and crinkled. He cleared his throat about five times before he finally spoke.

'Uh, I just came over to say I was sorry,' he said. 'Real sorry.'

I set the grocery bag full of dye bottles on the sidewalk. My sister stood behind me and said, 'Is this some kind of sick joke?'

'No way.' Bull shook his head forcefully. 'I'm right-eously sorry – for everything, dude.'

He was looking straight at me. 'All the times me and Jasper hassled you, it was wrong, OK? Bogus and wrong.'

'What's going on, Bull?'

'Nothin'! Why you ask me that?'

'Because all of a sudden you're Mister Huggy Bear. It's very weird.'

'Come on, Underwood, can't a dude say he's sorry and be real? What's the problem?'

Bull was getting frustrated, and I didn't want to push him too far. 'OK, we're cool,' I said. 'You say you're sorry, I believe you.'

'Excellent.'

'Well, *I* don't believe you,' Abbey cut in. 'Either you're faking it, or you've had a total personality trans-plant.'

Bull's long, dull face pinched in confusion. 'Whaddya mean by that? What kind a "transplant" you say?'

'Never mind,' I said. 'What about Jasper Jr?'

'Oh yeah, I almost forgot. He's sorry, too.'

'Really? Then where is he?'

Bull hitched his shoulders. Dark half-moons of sweat had appeared in the armpits of his faded Harley-Davidson T-shirt.

'He couldn't come, but he wanted me to tell you it won't never happen again,' Bull said. 'We won't beat on you no more.'

'That's nice. Next you'll be sending me flowers.' Naturally, Bull didn't catch on that I was being sarcastic.

'I'd really like to hear Jasper Jr's apology in person,' I said.

'Fat chance,' mumbled my sister. She picked up the grocery bag and lugged it inside the house.

Bull just stood there, sweating through his shirt and staring down at his enormous bare feet. It sounds strange, but I felt sort of sorry for the guy. He'd quit school and left the Keys to be a big baseball star, but here he was back on the rock, bagging groceries and hanging out with losers like Jasper Jr.

'Come on, man. Tell the truth,' I said, though it wasn't in Bull's nature.

He looked up slowly. 'Underwood, who's the freaky old man? The guy in the woods?'

'Just a friend,' I said, thinking: A friend and total stranger.

'Where'd he get that wicked-bad scar on his face?'

'He doesn't talk about it,' I said, hoping that Bull would think I was tight with the pirate guy.

'Thing is,' Bull said, 'he told me and Jasper to . . . well—'

'What?'

'He told us to tell you we was sorry for what we done to you and your little sister. He was real clear on that,' Bull said. 'But when it come time, Jasper just flat wouldn't do it. He said he didn't care what some crazy old bush rat told him.'

'What else did the old man in the woods say?' I asked.

Bull turned and checked over his shoulder, his eyes moving up and down the street. 'He said not to screw up again. He said he'll be hangin' close, and don't never forget it.'

Bull's visit finally made sense. He'd come to apologize because he was terrified not to.

'You'll tell him, won't you, Underwood? Tell him I stopped over and said I was sorry. When you see him again, I mean.'

'Sure, Bull. When I see him again.'

Though I wondered if I ever would.

After lunch my sister and I headed for Shelly's place to deliver the food dye and review our plan. Even though she came to the door wearing the nappy pink robe and carrying a plastic razor, we could tell that she was in better shape than the day before.

She waved us inside and cheerfully resumed shaving her legs at the kitchen sink, a procedure I'd never

witnessed so up close and personal. The way Shelly
did it wasn't quite as glamorous as in the TV com-
mercials. Whenever she nicked herself, she'd cuss like
a biker and wipe away the blood with her pinkie.
Abbey watched in fascination but I felt kind of weird,
so I turned away and pretended to be enchanted by
the scummy aquarium. I could hear the razor blade
scraping across Shelly's skin as she said, 'So – we're
good to go?'

'What about Billy Babcock?' I asked.

'Don't worry, I got that all figured out.'

But I *was* worried.

If Billy was at the coast guard station when the sewage
spill was reported, he'd tip off Dusty Muleman right
away. It wouldn't take long for Dusty's crew to unhitch
the *Coral Queen* and take her offshore, where they
could flush the holding tank until there was no trace of
our dye – and no way to connect Dusty to the crime.

'Ever since he heard Lice was gone, Billy's been
spendin' lots of time at my bar,' Shelly said, 'leaving
ten-dollar tips on ten-dollar tabs.'

'Did he ask you out?' Abbey said.

'Only about two or three times a night.' Shelly
tossed the plastic razor into a trash basket, poured
herself a cup of coffee, and sat down at the dinette.

'I'll handle Billy Babcock,' she said with a confi-
dent smile. 'Now lemme see what you got.'

Abbey gave her the grocery bag containing the bottles of colouring gel. Shelly peeked inside and said, 'Those are puny little suckers. Sure that'll do the job?'

'Well, it's concentrated—' I started to explain.

'I *know* it's concentrated, Noah. I've baked a few treats in my time.'

Abbey told her that we'd bought out the store. 'Thirty-four bottles. Is that OK?'

'No problem,' Shelly said. 'I've got a purse big enough to carry a Honda Civic.' She held up one of the bottles. 'Ever use this stuff before?'

Abbey and I shook our heads.

'Well, it doesn't pour out like water. It's more gooey, like sunblock, so you've really gotta squeeze,' Shelly said, demonstrating on a capped container. 'Thirty-four bottles, that's gonna take some time.'

I hadn't thought about that when we'd picked out the gel. Neither had Abbey.

'See, it's just me working solo behind the bar,' said Shelly, 'and Dusty doesn't like his customers to go thirsty. I only get two fifteen-minute potty breaks every night, which ain't nearly enough time to flush all this stuff.'

'Does that mean you can't help us?' I asked.

'Now don't get your shorts in a knot,' she said. 'I'll tell Dusty I got sick off the shrimp salad – what's he gonna do, make me go in a bucket?'

'Isn't there a head near the bar?' I asked.

Abbey poked me. 'A what?'

'A toilet,' I explained. 'On ships they're called heads.'

Shelly told us that the *Coral Queen* had three sets. 'One fore, one aft, and one up in the wheelhouse, which is out of the question. It's only for the casino manager and the crew.'

'But aren't you part of the crew?' Abbey said.

'No, sweetie, I'm a bartender. They make me tinkle with the civilians.'

The more I heard, the more worried I got. The longer that Shelly was away from the bar, the greater the risk that Dusty or one of his goons would go searching for her. Other things could go wrong, too. What if the toilet she was using malfunctioned, or got clogged?

I decided on a slight change of plan.

'You'll need some backup on board,' I said. 'I'll take half the dye and flush it from a different head.'

Shelly tossed her head. 'Oh no you don't, James Bond Jr. It's too hairy.'

'Just find me a place to hide. There's got to be somewhere safe.'

'Hello? What about me?' Abbey interjected.

Together Shelly and I turned and said: 'No way!'

'You don't bring me along, I'll rat you out to Dad

and Mom,' my sister declared. 'I swear to God, Noah.'

She wasn't joking, either. The veins in her scrawny neck were popping out, she was so ticked off.

'You couldn't do this without me,' she said. 'If it wasn't for my fifty-one bucks, you wouldn't have enough dye to colour a birdbath!'

I couldn't argue with that.

'This is gettin' way too complicated,' Shelly said, slurping at her coffee.

'Look, we're only going to get one chance at Dusty,' I said, 'so we'd better do it right.'

Shelly shot me a doubtful look. 'If you two brats get caught—'

'We won't,' Abbey cut in.

'But if you do—'

'We'll never mention your name,' I said. 'That's a promise.'

'Double promise,' said Abbey.

Shelly sighed. 'I must be outta my mind.'

It was almost five-thirty when Mr Shine dropped off my parents at the house.

They'd spent the afternoon at the courthouse, working out the final settlement of the *Coral Queen* case. Dusty Muleman had agreed not to prosecute my father for scuttling the casino boat, and in exchange Dad had promised to pay back Dusty's insurance company for the cost of refloating the thing, cleaning it up, and fixing the diesels. The bill must have been super expensive because the judge gave my father five whole years to pay it off. He also made Dad swear not to say anything bad about Dusty on TV, in the newspapers, or anywhere in public.

'So much for the First Amendment,' my father griped as we sat down to dinner. 'Might as well walk around with a cork in my mouth.'

'The important thing is, it's over,' Mom said. 'Now maybe our lives can get back to normal.'

I didn't dare look at Abbey for fear of cluing my mother that we were up to something. Dad was too bummed out to notice.

'Everybody in the county thinks I'm crazy anyway,' he said sourly.

'Who cares what everybody thinks?' I said.

'And who cares if you're crazy,' Abbey piped up, 'as long as it's a *good* crazy.'

She meant that as a compliment, and my father seemed to take it that way. 'It's unholy what Dusty is doing, a crime against nature,' Dad went on. 'Know what he deserves? He deserves to be—'

'Paine, that's enough,' my mother said sternly. 'Someday he'll get exactly what he deserves. What goes around comes around.'

Dad snorted. 'If only.'

'Mom's right,' Abbey said. 'Dusty can't get away with this stuff for ever.'

My sister played it perfectly straight. She's a slick little actress.

'Someday they're going to bust him cold. Don't worry,' she said.

Dad looked at her fondly and said, 'Let's hope you're right.' But we could tell he didn't believe that Dusty Muleman would ever be caught.

My mother said, 'Noah, we need you to stay home with Abbey tomorrow night.'

'What for?' I tried to sound annoyed but I was really excited. This was the golden chance that my sister and I needed.

'Your dad and I are going out for dinner and a movie,' Mom said.

'Woo-hoo, a hot date!' teased Abbey.

'We're celebrating your father's new job.'

'Oh yeah,' Dad said dryly. 'My exciting new career, towing numskull tourists off the bonefish flats.'

'Well, doesn't it beat driving a cab?' I asked.

'True enough,' he admitted.

'I want you both in bed by eleven. Not a minute later,' Mom told us. 'You hear me?'

'Absolutely,' I said.

'Double absolutely,' said Abbey. 'Eleven sharp.'

Neither of us could look Mom in the eye. It felt lousy lying to her, but honestly we had no choice. Not if we hoped to catch Dusty Muleman red-handed.

Or fuchsia-handed, to be exact.

FIFTEEN

Mom and Dad left on their 'hot date' at exactly a quarter to seven. The *Coral Queen* opened for business at eight, so Abbey and I didn't have a moment to spare.

We rode out bikes to Rado's house and jumped the wooden fence, which turned out to be a real bad idea. Rado and his parents were still vacationing in Colorado (which I knew), but they'd left Godzilla at home in the backyard (which I didn't know).

Godzilla isn't the world's smartest dog, but he's the biggest I've ever seen. Rado says he's 'part rottweiler, part Newfoundland, and part grizzly bear'. He easily outweighed my sister and me put together, and he wasn't all that happy to see us.

'Good dog,' I said in the calmest voice I could fake.

'Nice try,' whispered Abbey, 'but we're still gonna die.'

Godzilla had cornered us against the fence, and we didn't dare make a move. I was hoping the beast remembered me although it probably wouldn't matter, if the neighbours had forgotten to feed him. Abbey would be the appetizer and I'd be the main course.

'Here, boy,' I said, holding out my right hand.

'Are you crazy?' Abbey hissed.

'Dogs never forget the smell of a person they've met.'

'Says who?'

'Says the *Animal Planet*, that's who. They did a whole show on dogs' noses,' I said.

'Yeah, well, obviously you missed the episode on dogs' teeth.'

But Godzilla didn't chomp off my hand. He sniffed it suspiciously and nudged it with his moist snout. I'd be lying if I said I wasn't shaking.

'Noah, his tail's not wagging,' Abbey said under her breath.

'Thanks for the bulletin.'

'If he bites you, I'm biting him.'

'Easy, girl,' I said.

They say you can look into a dog's eyes and know whether he's friendly or not. Unfortunately, I couldn't see Godzilla's eyes because they were hidden beneath thick tangles of black Newfoundland hair. A pearly string of drool hung from his mouth, which meant he was either hot or hungry, or possibly both.

With my left hand I fished into my pants and took out a green apple that I'd brought along for a snack.

Abbey grunted. 'Noah, you've *got* to be kidding. Dogs don't eat fruit!'

'It's the best I can do, unless you've got a sirloin steak in your backpack.' I held out the apple and said, 'Here, boy. Yum!'

Godzilla cocked his anchor-sized head and let out a snort.

'It's a Granny Smith,' I said, as if he actually understood. 'Go on and try it. It tastes good.'

'Yeah, if you're a squirrel,' my sister muttered.

But to our total amazement the huge dog opened his huge jaws and clamped down his huge fangs on the apple, which he firmly tugged from my trembling hand.

As Godzilla trotted away with his prize, I said to Abbey, 'Check out his tail.'

It was wagging cheerfully.

Abbey and I hurried toward the canal, where Rado kept a blue dinghy tied to the sea wall. His father had salvaged the little boat off a scuttled motor yacht and patched up the fibreglass as good as new. It wasn't more than ten feet long, but it was dry and sturdy, with high sides and a deep hull. Rado, Thom, and I often took it out on calm days to snorkel around the bridges.

When we climbed into the dinghy, I tossed Abbey one of the life vests. She insisted she didn't need it, but I told her we weren't going anywhere until she put it on.

Next I gave her a quick lesson on cranking the outboard motor. It was an ancient little Evinrude that could be stubborn before it warmed up. I showed Abbey how to use both hands to yank the starter cord, which was tricky. If you didn't let go in time, the pullback could wrench you off balance and spin you overboard.

After a half dozen hard tugs, the motor spluttered to life in a burp of purple smoke. Rado's dad always made sure the gas can was full, but I checked anyway, just in case. Getting stranded would be a total disaster.

My sister moved to the front of the dinghy and untied the bow rope. I unhitched the ropes and shoved off.

'Ready?' I asked her.

'Absolutely,' she said, and flashed me a double thumbs-up.

As we cruised slowly toward the mouth of the canal, I glanced back and saw Godzilla watching us from the sea wall. He barked once, but the noise was muffled by the juicy green apple still clenched in his jaws.

Growing up near the ocean, you learn about some strange superstitions. For instance, lots of fishing captains won't let you bring a ripe banana on board because they believe it's bad luck. Nobody knows how that one got started, but Dad told me it's been around the docks since before Grandpa Bobby's time.

Another superstition is that dolphins bring good luck, so I was glad to spot a school of them herding baitfish as Abbey and I motored up the shoreline. By counting the dorsal fins, we figured out there were six grown-up dolphins and one baby – and they were having a blast, zipping in frothy circles, tossing mullets high in the air. I don't know if they're really a good omen, but seeing wild dolphins always makes me feel better. Any other time I would have stopped the boat to watch them play, but Abbey and I were in a hurry.

It stays light pretty late during the summer, so it was a clear ride to Dusty Muleman's marina. By the time we reached the channel markers, the waves had gotten choppy. I nosed the dinghy into some mangroves, cut the engine, and hopped out, balancing in my skateboard shoes on the slick rubbery roots. My sister dug through her backpack and took out a bottle of Gatorade, some bug spray, a Lemony Snicket book, and a flashlight. Then she handed the backpack to me.

'Sure you're OK with this?' I asked. 'I'll be gone a while.'

'Oh, gimme a break,' Abbey said. ''Course I'm OK.'

'Stay right here until you hear me yell "Geronimo!" Then you know what to do.'

'Why Geronimo?' she asked.

'Because I saw somebody do that in a movie once.'

'What the heck does it mean?'

'It means, "Hurry up and rescue me before I get my butt kicked by Dusty's big ugly goon,"' I said. 'No more questions, OK? Keep out of sight and I'll see you later.'

As I began working my way toward the docks, I heard Abbey call out, 'Be careful, Noah!'

I waved over my shoulder, but I didn't look back.

By the time I broke free of the mangroves, my shoes were soaking wet and my shins were scraped from the barnacle-covered roots. Crouching low, I dashed across a clearing and ducked behind Dusty Muleman's ticket shed. There on the ground, side by side, were the two large crates that Shelly had told me to look for.

Peeking around a corner of the shack, I saw that the parking area was filling up with cars. Customers were already lined up to board the *Coral Queen*. There weren't any kids in the crowd because kids weren't allowed on the casino boat; that's why I had to be so careful.

Using the sharp edge of a rock, I pried the lid off the first wooden crate. It was full of liquor bottles – rum from Haiti, according to the labels. Silently I replaced the cover and moved to the other crate.

As Shelly had promised, it was empty. I squeezed inside and dragged the heavy lid back into place. In order to fit I had to lie flat and pull my knees to my chest. Abbey's backpack, stuffed with containers of food dye, served as a lumpy pillow under my head. I was so cramped it felt like I was hiding in one of those magician's boxes, pretending to be disappeared.

The crate was dark and musty inside. At first I was afraid I couldn't breathe, but soon I felt whispers of air seeping under the lid. I took a few gulps, closed my eyes, and began to wait.

Before long I heard the scuff of footsteps and then the low sounds of men talking. The first voice I didn't recognize, but the thick accent of the second one was unmistakable: it was Dusty's bald gorilla, Luno.

The men grunted as they hoisted the first crate and hauled it off to the *Coral Queen*. By the time they returned my heart was thumping like a jackhammer. Luno lifted one end of my crate while his companion grabbed the other. I went rigid and held my breath. I could hear them swearing and complaining about the weight.

With every step, the crate tipped and lurched and

bounced. I knew I'd be dead meat if the lid fell off, so I dug my fingernails into the wooden slats to keep it in place.

Finally, the goons set me down with a jolting thud, and I knew I was on the boat. Once they were gone, I seriously thought about kicking my way out of that miserable wooden tomb. I could have done it, no problem, except that I'd promised Shelly to stay put until she got there.

So I waited some more.

And waited. And waited.

The *Coral Queen* was getting noisy as the customers piled aboard. Nobody else came near the crate, though, so I figured I must be in a storage area behind a wall or a door. Wherever it was, there was definitely no air-conditioning.

Before long I was sweating like a horse, and my throat was as dry as sawdust. I wondered how much longer I could stand it inside that mouldy old box.

It seemed like I was cooped up for hours, but it probably wasn't even twenty minutes before Shelly tapped three times on the side. She helped me climb out and handed me a cold bottle of water – nothing in my whole life had ever tasted so good. I hugged her, tangerine perfume and all. That's how grateful I was.

She put a finger to her lips and motioned for me

to follow. It was impossible not to notice that she was wearing those wild fishnet stockings and tippy high-heeled shoes that made her about five inches taller than normal. She led me along a dim corridor that opened onto one of the busy casino decks. The noise hit me like a roar – the slot machines clanging, people laughing and hooting, some lame calypso band mangling a Jimmy Buffett song.

'There it is, Noah.' Shelly pointed to a door. On it hung a hand-carved sign that spelled out the word 'MERMAIDS'.

'Don't move,' she told me, and promptly disappeared into the stall. Seconds later the door cracked open, and Shelly's blonde head poked out. She looked around warily, then signalled for me to join her.

Inside the ladies' restroom.

So I did. The two of us could barely fit.

'Where's the stuff?' she whispered.

I patted Abbey's backpack. The day before, Shelly and I had divided the stash of food colouring: seventeen bottles for me, seventeen for her.

'You got the sign?' I asked.

She smiled and held it up for me to see: a square piece of cardboard on which she had printed in capital letters with a jet-black marker: OUT OF ORDER.

'Guaranteed privacy,' she assured me.

'But what about you?' I was worried that she

wouldn't have a safe place to flush her supply of the dye.

'There's another Mermaids' john up front. I'll use that one for my potty breaks.'

'But what if somebody's already in there?' I asked.

'Then I'll crash the Mermen's.'

'The men's room? You serious?'

Shelly shrugged. 'Hey, who's gonna stop me?'

She had a point. 'I gotta get back to the bar,' she said 'Billy Babcock's waitin' on me all moony-eyed. Poor sap thinks he's in love.' She gave my shoulder a friendly tweak. 'Good luck, young Underwood.'

'You, too, Shelly.'

I locked the door the instant it closed. As soon as I heard her tack up the OUT OF ORDER sign, I unzipped Abbey's backpack and removed the dye bottles.

The head on a boat is basically a glorified closet, with barely enough room to sit and do your business. This one smelled like a mixture of stale beer, Clorox bleach, and Shelly's fruity perfume, but it was still less obnoxious than most public commodes.

And as uncomfortable as it was, it was way better than being sealed up inside a liquor crate.

For a moment I wondered what my father would have thought if he could see me there, locked in the Mermaids' head on the *Coral Queen*. The parent part of him would have been mad at me for sneaking aboard, while the nature-loving part of him would have been proud of me for trying to nail Dusty Muleman.

Knowing Dad, he would've had one firm piece of advice: *Don't get caught!*

When I opened the first bottle of food colouring, I saw that Shelly was right. The gel oozed out like molasses. Carefully I squeezed the plastic container until every gooey purple drop landed in the toilet hole.

Then I gave a good hard flush to make sure the dye went where it was supposed to go. Shelly had warned me that the stuff could get gummy pretty quick. If it stuck in the plumbing pipes, our plan would be ruined.

There was only one way to check it out. I knelt down, pinched my nose, and peered into the nasty depths of the head. Not a speck of fuchsia could be seen.

So far, so good.

One bottle down, sixteen to go.

Time passes incredibly slowly when you're trapped in a restroom.

Whenever I got ready to make a break, people would stop in loud groups outside the door – talking, laughing, singing along to the music.

I was dying to get out of there, but I had to be patient. I had to wait for a lull.

I kept thinking of Abbey, alone in Rado's dinghy, reading her book by flashlight. Even though there were no dangerous wild animals in the mangroves, I was afraid she might get spooked by some of the freaky night noises. If you've never heard two raccoons fighting before, you'd swear it was a chainsaw massacre.

When I wasn't worrying about my sister, I was thinking about what else was happening on board the *Coral Queen*. With so much partying, the other toilets were probably getting flushed nonstop. If Dusty Muleman pulled his usual trick, all that raw waste would be streaming out of the basin later.

It made me mad, which was good. I needed to stay mad in order to do what I had to. Every two or three minutes I looked at my watch, wondering why the hands weren't moving faster.

Mom and Dad were probably still at dinner. Afterward they were supposed to go to a late movie in Tavernier. That meant they'd be home around twelve-thirty, so Abbey and I had to be back at the house and in bed before then.

The *Coral Queen* closed at midnight. If I waited until then to slip away, we'd have less than thirty minutes to run the dinghy back to Rado's dock, grab our bikes, and race home. I didn't like the odds because it was dark on the water and the dinghy was slow. I also didn't like the idea of three more hours in the ladies' room.

I decided to make a run for it, crowds and all, and pray that nobody would try to catch me. Shelly had said that most of the regular customers were so heavy into the gambling that a rhinoceros could get loose on board and they wouldn't care. I hoped she was right.

Quietly I gathered up the empty dye bottles – the only evidence that could ever incriminate me – and stowed them in Abbey's backpack.

But as I reached out and unlocked the door, the metal handle began to jiggle violently. Somebody was trying to get into the head.

I grabbed the handle with both hands and braced my shoes against the sink.

'Hey, open up!' demanded a croaky female voice. 'I gotta go!'

Either she didn't see the OUT OF ORDER sign, or she was so desperate that it didn't matter. From outside came a heavy grunt, and the handle was nearly yanked from my grip.

The door opened no more than two inches, but it was enough to give me a startling peek at the intruder. She looked about eighty-five in both age and weight, which wasn't what I expected. She was pulling so ferociously on the door that I wouldn't have been surprised to see a three-hundred-pound sumo wrestler on the other side.

'You open up right this second!' the old woman squawked. 'I gotta go now!'

She wore a shiny copper-coloured wig that fit like a helmet. Her face was caked with powdery make-up, and her sparkly fake eyelashes were longer than a camel's. A cigarette dangled from parrotfish lips that were puffy and painted the colour of sliced mangoes.

'Can't you read the sign?' I asked through the crack.

'*What* sign, Einstein?'

That's when I spotted the piece of cardboard between her feet on the scuffed floor. Shelly's tack must have come loose.

'Hey, you're not even a Mermaid!' the old woman snapped, spitting her cigarette. 'Get outta that bathroom 'fore I call Security.'

It took all my strength to pull the door shut.

'You little sicko!' She let out a string of cuss words that would have put my Grandma Janet into cardiac arrest.

'Go away,' I pleaded. 'This is an emergency.'

'Emergency? I'll show you a damn emergency.' The parrotfish lady pounded at the flimsy door with her bony fists. 'My bladder's about to blow like Mount Saint Helen, you hear me, young man?'

Now she was shouting like a maniac. I knew it wouldn't be long before a crew member came running to see what was wrong.

'Listen up, you brat,' the woman said. 'I'm gonna count to five and then I'm bustin' in – and you better not be sittin' on that john when I do. You read me, junior? It ain't gonna be pretty.'

'Please don't,' I said, but it was hopeless.

'One! Two! . . .'

There was no other choice. I stood up from the toilet, put on the backpack, and lowered one shoulder. When the nasty old buzzard barked 'Five!' I crashed out the door, ducked under her flailing, twig-sized arms, and took off running.

Nobody would've paid much attention if she hadn't started shrieking: 'Catch him! Catch that rotten little pervert!'

Luckily, I'm pretty fast and not real tall, so I was able to dodge and weave through the legs of the gamblers. A few of them glanced up, and one or two actually made a lame grab for my shirt. Fortunately, most of them had been celebrating hard and were in no condition to chase after me.

Shelly's eyes got as wide as saucers when I flew past the bar. A bleary, leathery-faced man who I assumed was Billy Babcock spun on his stool and exclaimed, 'Is that a *kid* on the boat?'

I headed topside. An angry yell rose from behind me, and I turned to see two humungous guys in hot pursuit. They looked seriously ticked off. Each wore a tight red T-shirt with the words EVENT STAFF silk-screened across the front.

Shelly had warned me about them – the bouncers.

They bellowed at me to stop, but that wasn't going to happen. I scampered to the upper deck and ran straight for the bow. Reflected below, in the glassy basin, were the twinkling, Christmassy lights of the *Coral Queen*.

It was a long way down to the water; longer than I'd imagined.

'Game's over,' a voice said.

I turned to face the bouncers, 400-odd pounds of meat and muscle. Panting from the chase, they wore cocky grins. They thought they had me cornered, but they were wrong.

One of them beckoned with a beefy finger. 'Let's go, boy.'

I kicked off my shoes and stuffed them into Abbey's backpack.

The other one spoke up: 'Chill out, shrimp. Don't try anything stupid.'

After that 'shrimp' remark, I couldn't resist messing with them. 'If I fall overboard and drown,' I said, 'you guys are in deep trouble.'

'Yeah, right.'

'My mom and dad'll sue Mr Muleman for every cent he's got, so you'd better watch it.'

The bouncers looked at each other and their smiles faded.

While they huddled to discuss their next move, I ducked under the railing and edged into position. I purposely didn't look down again.

One of the goons took a step toward me. 'Whaddya think you're doin'? You nuts?' he asked.

They were getting ready to rush me, I could tell.

'Move away from there!' ordered the other bouncer, also moving forward. 'You're gonna break your fool neck.'

'I wasn't planning on it,' I said.

Something like panic showed in their pudgy, squinting faces. They figured they'd lose their jobs, or worse, if they let something bad happen to me.

One of the men whipped out a walkie-talkie and held it close to his mouth. 'Luno! Better come check this out!'

'Yeah, tell him to hurry,' the other man said. 'This kid's a real space case.'

It was definitely time to go.

The bouncers reached out and lunged, but I was already in the air, falling sweetly to freedom.

Or so I told myself as I hollered, 'Geronimo!'

SIXTEEN

I don't remember hitting the water, but I do remember sinking.

Not very deep, but deep enough to remind me that I was wearing Abbey's backpack.

I could have ditched it, but that would have been the same as littering. Besides, MS ABBEY UNDERWOOD was written with a bright red marker in two different places on the backpack. If somebody found it and saw all those empty food-colouring bottles, we were busted for sure.

Hurriedly I loosened one strap of the backpack to free my right shoulder, which made it easier to swim. I wasn't breaking any Olympic records, but I was definitely putting some distance between myself and the *Coral Queen*. At any moment I expected the blue dinghy to come chugging into view, Abbey riding to the rescue.

Behind me, where the casino boat was moored, a shouting match had erupted. I turned my head and spotted Luno stomping back and forth under the dock lights, hollering furiously at the two bouncers on the top deck. The bouncers were yelling back, pointing across the basin.

Pointing at me, of course.

I kicked harder, thinking: Hurry up, Abbey. *Hurry.*

'Stop, boy!' Luno commanded. 'You stop now!'

He was running along the docks, trying to keep even with me, so I dove beneath the surface. The dirty water stung my eyes and I squeezed them shut. It didn't matter, because even with my eyes wide open I couldn't have seen a whale three inches in front of my nose – not in that murky basin in the dead of night. I was swimming blind, but at least I was swimming.

When I came up for air, a white blast of light caught me squarely in the face.

'There he is!' Luno cried out. He was standing on a fish-cleaning table, sweeping a portable spotlight across the basin.

I ducked like a turtle and swam farther. When I popped up again, the same thing happened – the bright light, Luno yelling at me to stop. This time, though, he sounded closer.

Where was my sister?

The channel was at least a hundred yards away. Luno would run out of dock before I'd run out of water, but I was getting exhausted. My clothes were slowing me down, and the waterlogged backpack felt heavier by the minute.

Still no sign of the dinghy.

Even if my 'Geronimo!' wasn't loud enough, Abbey surely must have heard Dusty Muleman's goons bellowing like bull elephants. I took a gulp of air and dove under again. Two kicks later I struck what seemed to be a wall of blubber.

A wall that moved.

Next thing I remember was me spinning like a top – then shooting upward, launched by some invisible brute force. Flying out of the water, I opened my eyes just in time to see an enormous brown shape, mossy and slick, pushing away at an incredible speed. A broad rounded tail slapped the surface so hard, it sounded like a rifle.

Right away I knew what had happened: I'd crashed into a sleeping manatee.

I splashed down in a tumble. For a solid minute I trod water, not going anywhere, until my heart quit racing and I was able to catch my breath. The marina was momentarily quiet except for the merry chime of steel drums from the *Coral Queen*'s calypso band.

Where in the world was Abbey? And where was that caveman Luno?

I began swimming again, although not as bravely as before. The collision with the sea cow had rattled me – I couldn't help wondering what other creatures might be cruising around the dark cloudy basin. As huge as manatees are, they feed strictly on vegetation and have no appetite for humans. That's not true for everything that swims at night, especially certain large and fearless sharks.

The water was as warm as soup, but an icy shiver ran down my neck as I kicked onward. I only know a few prayers by heart, but I said all of them to myself. *Twice.* That's how scared I was.

I can't say for certain whether God was listening, but it wasn't long afterward that I heard the wheezy *chug-a-chug-chug* of a small outboard motor. I stopped moving and fixed my eyes in the direction of the noise. A familiar shape took form along the edge of the shadows, near the mouth of the basin.

As the shape drew closer, into the pale wash of the dock lights, I recognized the blue dinghy and the spindly silhouette of my sister at the helm.

Excitedly I called Abbey's name, and she responded with our pre-arranged signal: three rapid blinks of her flashlight. I set out for the little boat as fast as I could, not caring how much noise I made. All I wanted was to get out of the water in one piece.

Abbey whistled, but I was too exhausted to whistle back. The dinghy was no longer heading my way; in fact, it seemed to be sliding away in the current. By the time I caught up, my arms and legs were starting to cramp. I grabbed onto the bow and, with my sister's help, hauled myself aboard.

At first I couldn't even talk – I just sat there, dripping and panting like a tired old dog. Finally, I shook off the backpack and dried my face with the tail of Abbey's shirt.

'You OK?' she asked.

I nodded and rubbed my aching muscles. 'How come you turned off the engine?'

'I didn't,' Abbey said. 'It stalled out.'

'Nice.'

'That's how come I was late getting here. It took like for ever to get the stupid thing started!'

I stepped to the stern to confront the creaky old Evinrude. The starter cord was a three-foot length of rope that wrapped tightly around the engine's flywheel. A small block of plastic served as a handle on the exposed end of the rope, so you could pull it without shredding your fingers.

Hand-cranking an outboard is harder than starting a lawn mower. Marine engines have more horsepower, so it takes more strength to turn the flywheel. After bracing my heels against the transom of the dinghy, I locked both hands around the grip of the starter cord.

'Do it,' said my sister.

'Keep your fingers crossed.'

I reared back and yanked. The engine shuddered, coughed once, then went silent.

'Crap,' mumbled Abbey.

'Don't worry,' I said, which was ridiculous. Only an idiot wouldn't have been worried.

I shifted my weight slightly and took hold of the rope again.

'Let it happen, cap'n,' said Abbey.

At that instant the dinghy lit up like a movie stage – Luno had found us with his spotlight. Abbey and I shielded our eyes and tried to see where he was. His voice gave us the answer: he was close.

Too close.

'You again!' we heard him snarl. 'You two punks! This time you no get away!'

He was standing at the end of the last dock in the marina. Off our port side was the mouth of the basin and, beyond that, open sea. If I could only get Rado's darn engine started, Abbey and I could escape.

Again I tried the starter cord, and again nothing happened but a sad sputter.

'We're drifting toward the dock,' my sister said gloomily.

'I can see that.'

'Should we jump?'

'No, not yet.'

Four, five, six times I pulled the rope with the same depressing result. Meanwhile a breeze was pushing the dinghy steadily toward the dock, where Luno was pacing like a hungry cat. For amusement he would occasionally zap us with the hot beam of his spotlight.

Abbey crouched low in the bow, but I had to keep standing. It was the only way to put enough force into pulling the starter cord.

As we floated closer to the lights, we could make out Luno's gloating expression. His smile was thin and ugly.

Frantically I jerked on the starter cord, and this time the old engine gave an encouraging kick before sputtering out.

Luno crowed, 'I get you punks now!'

My sister poked me in the back. 'Noah, look! Quick!'

Another figure had joined the bald goon at the end of the dock. I recognized him immediately in that flowered Hawaiian shirt, but just the stink from his cigar would have given him away. It was Dusty Muleman himself.

'I'm outta here,' said Abbey, poised to jump.

'No, wait.' I feverishly resumed hauling on the starter cord, one hard pull after another. Nothing makes you forget how tired you are like pure cold fear. I was working like a robot in high gear.

Then my sister cried, 'Noah, duck!'

And ducking would have been a smart move, no doubt about it. Because I turned to see Luno with his meaty right arm extended, aiming a stubby-looking gun at the dinghy. Dusty stood off to the side, blowing lazy rings of blue smoke.

The scene was so unreal, I just froze. It was like watching someone else's nightmare. I felt blank and numb and far away.

'What's the matter with you? Get down!' Abbey yelled.

By now we'd drifted to within fifty feet of the dock, which made us an easy target. Finally an alarm bell went off in my brain and I threw up both arms, shouting, 'Don't shoot! We give up!'

Dusty chuckled quietly. Luno was leering like a psycho. He did not lower the gun barrel even one millimetre.

'You kids make bad mistake,' he said. 'Now must pay.'

If ever I was going to wet my pants in public, it would have been right then and there.

Yet all I could think about was protecting my sister, so I threw myself on top of her. The landing wasn't so graceful – I banged my chin on the gunwale and nearly capsized us. Wrapping my arms around Abbey, I waited for the explosion of a gunshot.

It never came. A fierce and breathless struggle had broken out on the dock. Peeking over the side of the dinghy, Abbey and I witnessed an amazing sight.

As if dropped from the stars, a third man had materialised under the dock lights – and he was pounding Luno into a sweaty lump of Jell-O. The only sign of Dusty Muleman was the slapping of his designer flip-flops against the ground as he scurried off in terror toward the *Coral Queen*.

The cheerful tinkle of steel drums now mixed with Luno's odd piggish grunts, the wiry stranger swinging a deck mop with painful accuracy.

In fact, he wasn't a total stranger to me and my sister. We were near enough to see the M-shaped scar on his weathered tan face, and the bright gold coin swinging from the chain around his neck.

'The pirate guy!' Abbey whispered gleefully. 'Outrageous!'

'Don't you move,' I told her, and clambered to the stern. I seized the handle of the starter rope and, from a squatting position, yanked with every ounce of muscle I had left.

By some small miracle, the rickety old engine purred to life.

I whipped the dinghy around, aimed it toward the channel, and twisted the throttle wide open. I glanced back just as the mysterious pirate was hurling Luno's stubby gun into the basin. For an old geezer, he had a pretty good arm.

After reaching the open water, I slowed to half speed. Running a boat at night is tricky because you can't see very far or very clearly, and a cheapo flashlight doesn't help much. All kinds of hazardous clutter could be floating in your path – boards, driftwood, coconuts, ropes – and it wouldn't have taken much to wreck the propeller blades on the old Evinrude.

Abbey perched on the bow, watching out for obstacles while I tried to navigate by the lights of the shoreline motels, mansions, TV parks, tiki bars. The darkest stretch was Thunder Beach, peaceful and deserted under a yellow moon. An ideal night for a momma turtle to crawl up and lay her eggs, I thought.

The salt air felt good on our faces as we ran against a light chop. Above us hung a glittering spray of stars that stretched all the way to Cuba. I was happier than I'd ever been, and so was Abbey.

'We did it!' she cheered. 'We are *so* hot!'

'*Adiós*, Captain Muleman!' I shouted with a phoney salute.

The hardest part of Operation Royal Flush was over. We'd laid the trap and escaped, though barely. Being chased by Luno wasn't part of the plan, but it didn't spoil anything. For now, Dusty Muleman and his gorillas wouldn't be able to figure out what I'd been doing aboard the *Coral Queen*, since the only clue had gone down the toilets.

Way, way down the toilets, into the holding tank – the last place they'd ever stick their heads.

Only later would Dusty realize what I'd done, and by then he'd have worse problems – namely the US Coast Guard, which I intended to call first thing in the morning. But as jazzed as I was, I couldn't forget how close Abbey and I had come to being shot. *Shot.* It was unbelievable.

Why, I wondered, would Dusty stand there and let Luno take aim at a couple of pint-sized trespassers? We must have really annoyed him, I thought, with all our snooping around.

And what were the odds of being rescued for a second time by the same stranger? Either the old pirate was following us around like some sort of weird guardian angel, or Abbey and I were the luckiest two kids in Florida.

'Hard right!' she called from the bow.

I pushed the tiller, and we skittered past a glistening spear of two-by-four, only inches away. It would have punched a hole in the hull for sure.

'Good eyes,' I called to my sister.

'Thanks. What's that noise?'

'Don't know.'

'Noah, why are you slowing us down?' she shouted.

'I'm not,' I said. 'Not on purpose, anyway.'

But the little boat was definitely losing speed. The loud noise that Abbey and I had heard was the outboard engine throwing a piston rod, though we didn't know that at the time.

The motor conked out with a sickly rattle.

I knew we were in major trouble, but I went through the motions of removing the cowling and fiddling with the spark-plug connections. It didn't fool Abbey for a second.

'I don't suppose you brought Dad's toolbox,' she said.

'Very funny.'

I tried to pull the starter cord, but it wouldn't budge. The old Evinrude was stone dead.

A heavy, tired silence fell over us. Once again the little boat was at the mercy of the breeze, which was taking us out to sea, toward the Straits of Florida. Obviously our good luck had run out.

'We're history,' my sister said. 'Mom and Dad'll go postal when they get home and we're not there.'

The wind was clocking around to the northwest. In summer that usually meant bad weather was on the way.

I said, 'Better toss the anchor – no, wait a second . . .'

Too late. My stomach clenched when I heard the splash.

'Let me guess,' Abbey said. 'The rope wasn't tied on, was it?'

'My fault. I should've checked.'

'So I just threw our anchor away. How nice.' She sighed in discouragement. 'Now what?'

We saw a distant flash of electric blue, which was followed by a slow deep rumble.

'Seven miles. Not good,' Abbey said.

Dad had taught us how to count the seconds between the lightning bolt and thunder – one thousand, two thousand, three thousand – to figure out how many miles away a storm was. Like Abbey, I'd counted seven.

'Maybe it'll miss us,' she said.

'Yeah.' And maybe someday monkeys will fly helicopters, I thought.

In a few short minutes our mood had plunged from the highest high to the lowest low. The moon slipped behind a rolling grey carpet of clouds, and the freshening gusts smelled wet. Abbey scrunched low in the bow while I hunkered between the seats.

The lightning got brighter and the thunder got louder, but all we could do was brace for it. Rado's dinghy had no oars, and we were already too far from shore to swim – not that either of us were eager to jump in. I remembered Dad saying that you always stay with a boat as long as it's still floating, because a boat is easier than a body for searchers to find.

Soon the wind began to hum, slapping us with sheets of cool rain.

'You all right?' I asked my sister.

'Snug as a bug,' she said.

The little boat slopped across the crests of the waves, moving farther and farther from shore. Stabs of lightning turned the dark into daylight, and I'd catch brief glimpses of Abbey, covering her face with the backpack. I felt horrible for getting us into such a mess, and I was furious at myself for letting her come along. It was one of the all-time dumbest things I'd ever done.

The wind-whipped raindrops stung our skin, and every thunderclap sounded like a bomb. As hard as I tried, I couldn't stop my knees from knocking against the hull. I didn't want Abbey to know how frightened I was, or how much danger we were in. If a lightning bolt struck the dinghy, we'd be roasted like crickets on a radiator.

I wiped off my wristwatch and checked the time: twenty minutes to one. Mom and Dad were home by now, probably going nuts trying to find us. I felt like throwing up.

'Hey, Noah?' Abbey said.

'What?'

'My butt's underwater.'

'Mine, too,' I said glumly.

'Shouldn't we, like, do something?'

'Yeah, I guess.'

We spent the next two hours bailing the boat, which is a major pain when all you've got are empty food-dye bottles that hold one measly ounce of liquid. Lucky for us, the storm blew through swiftly, the rain quit, and the dinghy didn't sink.

No sooner had the stars come out again than I heard Abbey snoring. I wasn't sure how far offshore we'd drifted, but I could still see the faint string of lights that marked the coastline. I stretched out on one of the seat planks, staring up at the moon and wondering how long it would take for somebody to spot us. I was determined to remain awake, in case a boat passed close by; then I could signal for help with the flashlight.

But my eyes didn't stay open very long. The next thing I remember was the sun warming my cheeks, a seagull squawking overhead – and something moist splatting in my hair.

One lousy little juice box.

'That's all we've got?' I said to Abbey. 'What happened to the Gatorade?'

'I drank it,' she said. 'I would've brought a whole cooler if I'd known we were getting lost at sea. Want some juice or not?'

She was still red in the face from laughing after the seagull crapped on my head – I thought she was going to have a total coronary. Then I almost fell overboard while dunking my hair in the water, trying to wash the poop out. Abbey thought *that* was really amusing, too.

And I guess it was. At least it kept our minds off the situation, which was getting more depressing by the minute.

I was happy to share the juice box, even though I usually can't stand fruit punch. When you're thirsty enough, you'll drink just about anything. It was only eight in the morning, and we were already damp with sweat. That's your basic July in the Florida Keys. By noon, I knew, we'd be in rough shape.

I was ticked at myself for not saving some of the rainwater we'd bailed from the boat. 'Remind me not to try out for *Survivor*,' I grumbled to Abbey.

She arranged the backpack on her head like a fat bumpy hat. 'I used to think Dad was the psycho in the family, but look at us!' she said. 'No water, no shade, no food, not even a fishing rod so we can catch something to eat.'

A small airplane passed overhead – the third one

of the morning – and we both stood up to wave. The plane circled once and then flew off, dashing our hopes again. From that altitude the dinghy must have looked like a blue dot on blue paper.

'Noah, when am I allowed to get scared?' Abbey tried to make it sound like she was kidding, but I could tell she was partly serious.

'At least we can still see the shore,' I said.

'So how deep's the water here?'

As we'd floated east, past the reef line, the colour had changed from turquoise to indigo. I didn't know the exact depth, but I guessed low on purpose.

'Fifty, maybe sixty feet. Not real deep.'

'Not for a tuna maybe,' said my sister, 'but way too deep for me.'

'Were you planning on taking a swim?'

'Yeah, me and the hammerheads.' She scanned the horizon and frowned. 'You said there'd be charter boats all over the place. You promised somebody would find us by nine o'clock.'

'Yeah, and there's still an hour left on my prediction.' I was trying not to sound as bummed as I was.

Miles away, we could see the blocky shape of a freighter steaming south, and a few deep-sea boats trolling back and forth. None of them were heading our way.

Not even close.

I tried to pull-start Rado's engine again, but it was no use. When I closed my eyes to take a break from the sun, I realized I was already thirsty again. My father says the summer heat in Florida is like the devil's oven, and that's about right.

Something started whining like a rusty hinge, and I looked up to spy another seagull circling the dinghy.

'Betcha five bucks he takes a dump on me, too,' I said.

Abbey managed a giggle. 'I'm safe under the backpack.'

It was amazing how calm and good-natured she was, considering the trouble we were in. Lots of people I know, grown-ups included, would've freaked out.

'I just thought of something,' she said. 'If we're stuck here on the boat, who's gonna call the coast guard on Dusty Muleman?'

'Good question.'

'Know what? This really bites.'

'Yeah, it does. I'm sorry, Abbey.'

'What for? We tried to stop something bad, and it didn't work. Doesn't mean we were wrong to try – Noah, are you listening to me?'

I wasn't.

'What are you staring at?' Abbey demanded.

'A boat,' I said, 'unless I'm so whacked out that

I'm imagining things. I swear it's coming this way.'

My sister shot to her feet.

'You see it, too?' I asked anxiously. 'Or is it a mirage?'

'Nope, it's the real deal.'

'Outstanding!'

We started waving and hollering like a couple of dweebs. This time, though, it actually worked. Pushing a frothy wake, the boat headed straight at us.

It wasn't a big one, maybe a twenty-four-footer, but it might as well have been the *Queen Elizabeth*. Abbey and I had never seen a more glorious sight.

Two figures, both of them hatless and wearing wraparound sunglasses, stood at the console under the T-top. As the boat drew closer, it slowed down and banked slightly, revealing large orange lettering on the side.

TROPICAL RESCUE, it said.

'Noah, is that who I think it is?' Abbey asked weakly.

'The one and only.'

'You want me to start sobbing and shaking?'

'Not yet,' I told her. 'First let's see how pissed off he is.'

'Is that Mom with him? Please tell me it's not Mom.'

'No, Abbey. Mom usually wears a shirt.'

We quit waving and cupped our hands to our eyes,

trying to see the bare-chested person through the glare.

With relief Abbey said, 'Oh good, it's a man.'

'Yeah, but guess who.'

'Who?'

'Check out the scar, Abbey.'

She gasped. 'This is *so* insane.'

The man riding with my father was the old pirate.

We were speechless as the towboat idled up to the dinghy. Dad tossed a rope, which I hitched to the bow cleat.

'Hey, guys,' my father said. 'Long night?'

We nodded lamely. The stranger stood next to Dad, smiling and fingering the gold coin on his neck. He seemed to be studying us closely.

Dad helped me and Abbey aboard the towboat. Then he pulled us close and squeezed like he might never let go.

'Are you two OK?' He examined us from head to toe, and seemed pleased to find no bullet holes, shark bites, or missing limbs.

'We're good,' I told him. 'Just a little thirsty, that's all.'

The old pirate guy handed each of us a cold bottle of water.

'Who *are* you?' Abbey asked him without even saying thanks. 'I'm sorry, but it's driving me crazy.'

The stranger took off his sunglasses and glanced over at Dad. It wasn't exactly a sad look, but there was something heavy about it.

'Kids,' said my father, 'say hello to your Grandpa Bobby.'

SEVENTEEN

'This is the US Coast Guard. Petty Officer Reilly speaking.'

'Yes, I'd like to report a boat dumping sewage in the water.'

'What's the name of the vessel?'

'It's called the *Coral Queen*.'

'The gambling boat? At the Muleman marina?'

'That's right.'

'Did you witness this violation personally?' Petty Officer Reilly asked.

'Look for a bright purple trail leading to Thunder Beach. But you'd better hurry!'

'Who am I speaking with?'

'Underwood. Paine Underwood.'

My second phone call was to the *Island Examiner* newspaper. This time I used my own name, not Dad's.

Miles Umlatt remembered me, of course.

'It's good to hear from you, Noah, but I'm sort of busy now. A bait truck just flipped over in Key Largo, and there's live shrimp all over the highway.'

'Want a real story? A front-page story?'

Miles Umlatt said, 'Sure, you bet.'

He was humouring me, playing along. I could picture the bored look on his pale splotchy face.

'All that stuff my dad said about Dusty Muleman? Well, it's true. Every word.'

Miles Umlatt said, 'I know how you must feel, Noah. If it were my father, I'd stick up for him, too—'

'You want proof? Get over to Dusty's marina right away.'

'Why? What's going on?' Suddenly he was interested.

'Ask the coast guard,' I said, and hung up.

Dad, Mom, and Abbey were in the living room, gathered around Grandpa Bobby. When I came out of the kitchen, he motioned for me to sit down beside him. For the first time I noticed his resemblance to my father – Dad was taller and heavier, but he had the same square chin and light green eyes.

Grandpa Bobby took out a small photograph, worn and creased from being folded and unfolded. In the picture, his curly hair was blond, not silvery, and there was no scar on his cheek. He was lifting some half-naked little kid high over his head. The kid was laughing and kicking his chubby white legs.

The kid was me.

'You were only two years old,' my grandfather said.

It was the first photograph of him that I'd ever seen. My parents had lost all their family albums when a tropical storm flooded our house on the night before my third birthday.

Grandpa Bobby passed the snapshot around. Then he carefully refolded it into a square and slipped it in his pocket. Turning back to me, he said, 'You wanna go first, champ?'

'No thanks. You go.'

He took a slow sip from a coffee mug. 'Lord, where do I start? I guess by sayin' how bad I feel for keepin' out of touch the last ten years or so.'

'Out of touch? Everybody thought you were dead!' Abbey exclaimed.

'I'm sorry, I truly am,' Grandpa Bobby said. 'Paine, Donna – believe me when I say I had good reasons for stayin' out of your life.'

I could tell that Mom and Dad were glad to have Grandpa Bobby back, but they were also kind of dazed and quiet. My sister wasn't dazed at all, since she'd never met him. He had disappeared before she was born.

'It's not a happy story,' he began. 'One day a man came along, said he needed a captain to make a couple of trips down to South America. The money was right, and I didn't ask many questions. Wasn't like I didn't know *what* to ask – I just chose not to. Anyways, the first run went fine. No problems with the second run, either. But the third time, oh man . . .'

'Were you smuggling drugs?' I asked. Even Abbey seemed shocked to hear me say it.

'No, champ, I've got no fondness for dopers. It was stones,' Grandpa Bobby said. 'Little green stones called emeralds. But smugglin' is smugglin', and stupid is stupid. And that's what I was – world-class stupid – because the guys I trusted turned out to be greedy, back-stabbin' liars. Actually, *face*-stabbin' liars.' He pointed ruefully at the M-shaped scar. 'Anyways, the details don't hardly matter. There was some serious ugliness, and yours truly had to go underground.'

Up close he didn't look so much like a pirate – at least not the kind of pirate you see in the movies. His teeth were too straight and his manners were too good.

But he also didn't look like the kind of grandpa you usually see in the movies. His belly was still flat and his muscles were hard, and he was brimming with some strange wild energy. You could tell he'd never spent a minute of his life dozing in a rocking chair.

Dad asked, 'What happened to the *Amanda Rose*?'

That was Grandpa Bobby's fishing boat, which he'd named after his wife, my grandmother. I never got to meet her because she passed away when my father was just a kid, about Abbey's age. Some sort of rare cancer, Mom told us. It was one of the only things my dad wouldn't talk about. Not ever.

'Paine, they stole the *Amanda Rose*,' my grandfather said sadly, 'the same night they tried to kill me. Ever since then I've spent every bleepin' minute trying to track down those rat bastards – pardon the language – and get back my boat.'

Mom spoke up. 'We kept getting different stories from the State Department. Somebody said your appendix ruptured. Somebody else said it was a bar fight.'

Grandpa Bobby slapped his gut. 'Far as I know, my appendix is fine and dandy. As for bar fights, well, who's countin'?'

'Then why'd they tell us you were dead when you weren't?' I asked.

'Because there was a dead American, Noah. They found him near a little village outside Barranquilla. My wallet happened to be in the man's pocket, so the Colombian cops figured that he was me,' Grandpa Bobby explained. 'That's the body your daddy's been writing letters to Washington about. The coffin never got dug up and shipped back to the States because I paid off a police captain to make sure it wouldn't.' He grinned slyly. 'See, I didn't want to miss my own funeral.'

Abbey folded her arms. 'Hold on. How did some dead guy end up with your wallet?'

'He stole it from me, which was a large mistake.' Grandpa Bobby took another sip of coffee. 'It tore me up on the inside, knowin' ya'll thought I was planted in some pauper's grave in the middle of nowhere. But I couldn't come back to Florida and bring the kind of trouble that was attached to me. You folks had a solid, decent life goin' here – young Noah gettin' started. Abbey on the way.'

'You could've called,' my sister said sharply. 'They've got telephones in South America, don't they?'

'Or sent a letter, at least,' I cut in, 'just to let Dad know you were OK.'

Grandpa Bobby sat back and smiled. 'Kids, lemme tell you somethin' about your daddy. He's a good man, but sometimes his brain takes a nap and lets his heart take the tiller.'

My father shifted uncomfortably. 'Oh, come on, Pop.'

But Grandpa Bobby was on a roll. He addressed Abbey and me directly. 'When your father was a boy, you know what his nickname was at school? "Pain-in-the-Butt" Underwood.'

Abbey and I busted out laughing.

'See, he had a bad habit of doing the very first thing that popped into his mind, no matter how foolish,' my grandfather said. 'Now, whaddya think he would've done if he'd found out I was still alive and scramblin' to stay that way, down in the jungles of Colombia? He would've hopped a plane or a boat or a donkey, whatever, and gone lookin' for me! Am I right, son? And likely gotten himself killed in the bargain.'

Dad stared down at his shoes.

My mother asked, 'So what made you come back, Pop?'

'This is first-rate coffee. Can I pour myself another cup?'

While Grandpa Bobby was in the kitchen, Abbey nudged my father and whispered: 'They really called you Paine-in-the-Butt? You are *so* busted.'

'Keep it up,' Dad said with a tight smile. 'I'll deal with you and your brother later.'

Grandpa Bobby returned with a full mug and a jelly doughnut. He took two bites of the doughnut and said, 'Here's what happened: I'm sittin' in a bar in this little harbour town, waitin' to meet up with some dock rat who claims he saw the *Amanda Rose* over in the Grenadines. Anyways, they love their satellite TV down there, and it so happens that this particular *cantina* picks up one of the Miami stations loud and clear.'

'Channel Ten?' I asked.

'That's right, Noah. So there I am, drinkin' a beer, mindin' my own business, when all of a sudden I look up and who do I see on the tube? Mr Paine Lee Underwood, my own son, your own daddy!'

Grandpa Bobby paused and shook his woolly head. 'He's wearin' the latest in jailhouse fashions, a nifty puke-orange jumpsuit, if I recall. And he's runnin' off at the mouth about why he sunk some jerk's boat, all because the man was dumpin' toilet poo into the water. My jaw dropped so far it damn near broke my kneecaps. There was my boy in jail!'

Dad looked up. 'Tell 'em what you did next, Pop.'

'You mean hitchin' a ride to Key West on that billionaire's yacht?'

'He didn't hitch,' my father said to me and Abbey. 'He stowed away.' Grandpa Bobby had already given Dad the full story, while they were out on the towboat searching for our dinghy.

'Where'd you hide?' Abbey asked.

My grandfather beamed. 'The wine locker, darlin'.'

'Perfect,' Mom said with a sigh.

'I didn't touch a drop, Donna, I swear,' Grandpa Bobby insisted. 'Anyways, I knew the Customs boys would sweep the yacht clean, once we docked in Key West. So as soon as we cleared the harbour, I went overboard. Swam to the Mallory docks and thumbed a ride north with a red-headed insurance adjuster who tried her best to save my heathen soul. She dropped me at Tavernier, where I made camp under the Snake Creek Bridge. Found a bunch of old newspapers there. Caught up on what was happening with Paine's court case.'

'Why'd you start tailing me and Abbey?' I asked.

'Just a hunch,' my grandfather said. 'In one of those papers was a story where they quoted you, Noah, talkin' about your father. You 'member that?'

'Hey, it wasn't *my* idea.' I shot a sour look at Dad.

'Well, you came off like a bright, sensible young fella. Still, I couldn't help thinkin' that if you were just a little too much like your daddy or granddaddy, you wouldn't sit still and let this Muleman creep get away with trashin' our family name, not to mention the Atlantic Ocean.' Grandpa Bobby winked, then inhaled the rest of his doughnut. 'So I decided to keep an eye on you and Miss Abbey, just in case you tried somethin' crazy.'

'Thank goodness you did,' Mom said.

My grandfather told us he'd been laying low during the day, fishing with a handline under the bridge. After sunset he'd hide out at the marina, waiting for us to make a move.

'Hiding where?' I asked.

'Last night it was the tuna tower of a big Bertram,' he said.

Abbey was delighted. 'I hid there, too! I even got video!'

'It's a long ways up,' Grandpa Bobby said, 'but a short trip down. That bald ape never knew what hit him.'

'His name's Luno,' I said.

'I don't care if his name is Mildred, I won't be sendin' him a get-well card.' Grandpa Bobby paused to finish his coffee.

Dad picked up the story. 'Mom and I got home from the movies around twelve-thirty. When we saw your beds were empty, we knew right away where you'd gone. She wanted to call the sheriff, but I said no way, I've had enough of their hospitality. So we hopped in the pickup, peeled out of the driveway, and there he was, larger than life—'

'In the middle of the road,' Mom said. 'No shirt, no shoes, dripping with sweat.'

'Flailing his arms and running straight at us,' Dad said, 'my old man!'

'What'd you do?' I asked.

'I turned very calmly to your mother and said, "Either that's a ghost, or the government's given us some bad information."'

Grandpa Bobby said he'd planned to keep his visit a secret – until he saw me and Abbey escape in the blue dinghy. The engine on that thing sounded like a bucket of nails in a blender. I knew you kids wouldn't get very far,' he said, 'so I ran and fetched your folks.'

'Wait a minute – you would've gone all the way back to South America without even saying hello?' Abbey was steaming. 'Without even letting us know you were alive? That's horrible.'

My grandfather sat forward and took one of her hands. 'Now listen here, tiger. All those years, there wasn't a day went by that I didn't want to pick up a phone and call your daddy. I missed him more than I can ever put into words.

'But it would've been wrong to drag him into the middle of my situation, which was deadly serious. So my plan was to sneak into the Keys on the sly and see what I might do behind the scenes. I brought along some cash for bail, lawyers, bribes, whatever. There was plenty more in a lockbox up in Hallandale, though I hear your Aunt Sandy and Uncle Del already helped themselves.'

Dad said, 'We don't need any money.'

Grandpa Bobby raised one silvery eyebrow. 'Really? Since when did you win the lottery?'

'We'll be fine,' Mom said warmly. 'But thank you, Pop.'

He smiled. 'I understand.'

'Well, *I* don't,' my sister grumbled. She snatched

her hand away from my grandfather. 'Know what I think? I think you're a big—'

'Abbey, knock it off,' I said. 'He saved our lives.'

'Not quite,' said Grandpa Bobby. 'Some private plane spotted your dinghy and called in the location. Your daddy had his VHF radio dialled to the coast guard's channel – turns out we were only about three miles away, so we beat the coasties no sweat. Your daddy's the one who knew where to search. I went along for the ride is all.'

'No, I'm not talking about the rescue,' I said, 'I'm talking about what happened on the docks – about Luno and the gun.'

My mother went stiff. 'What gun?'

'The guy was going to waste us!' Abbey burst out. 'I mean, we were *history*. Then Noah dived on top of me, and then he' – she nodded toward Grandpa Bobby – 'he jumped the goon and took the pistol away.'

Immediately I was sorry that I'd brought it up. My mom's face had gone white.

'He tried to kill you?' She looked at Grandpa Bobby. 'Is that true? He tried to kill the children?'

'Donna, it was a flare gun. He probably wanted to scare the you-know-what out of 'em,' my grandfather said.

'Just a *flare* gun?' Abbey sounded disappointed.

'It's still bad,' Dad said angrily. 'He could've set the dinghy on fire. Or your clothes.'

Grandpa Bobby told all of us to calm down. 'The main thing is, nobody got hurt except for Baldy. Now, I believe it's Noah's turn to tell us his story. You ready, champ?'

'I guess.'

My sister pretended to hold her nose. 'Don't leave out the part about the seagull,' she said.

I didn't leave out anything, even the stuff that made me look the opposite of brilliant. Nobody interrupted with questions. They just sat there and listened.

When I was finished, Dad clicked his teeth and said, 'You crashed into a manatee?'

Then Mom said, 'Who's this Shelly person?'

Then Abbey said, 'The Mermaids' bathroom? You perv!'

Then Grandpa Bobby stood up and took the chain from around his neck. He placed it in my hand and said, 'You earned it, Noah.'

The gold coin on the end of that chain was heavier than any coin I'd ever held. I couldn't believe he was giving it to me.

'Once belonged to the queen of Spain,' he said, 'about four hundred years ago.'

'Where'd you get it?' Dad asked.

'Won it in a dice game. Or maybe it was poker.'

Grandpa Bobby shrugged as if he honestly couldn't remember. 'Come on, troops, let's go for a ride.'

'Where to?' I asked.

'Thunder Beach,' he said. 'Where else?'

EIGHTEEN

The food colouring didn't show up as brightly in the sea as it did in the store bottles, but you could definitely see it. As Abbey and I had hoped, the current and the wind were in our favour, transporting the dye down the shoreline in a shiny stream from Dusty Muleman's basin.

Dad and Grandpa Bobby stood together on Thunder Beach, admiring the telltale trail of fuchsia.

'I'm impressed,' my father said. 'This was your idea, Noah?'

'Abbey's, too,' I said.

'All I did was pick out the colour,' she said.

'That's not true. We were fifty-fifty partners the whole way.'

My grandfather slapped a hand on Dad's shoulder. 'Paine, you and Donna really lucked out with these youngsters. They're true champs, both of 'em.'

'Most of the time,' Dad said, shooting us a sideways glance.

'You gotta admit,' said Grandpa Bobby, 'this is

a whole lot neater than sinkin' the man's boat.'

'Yeah, Pop, thanks for bringing that up.'

Mom kept staring at the purplish slick in the shallows. Even though she was wearing sunglasses, we could tell she was upset. At first I thought she was mad at Abbey and me, but it turned out that she wasn't. She was mad at Dusty Muleman.

'Unbelievable!' she exploded finally. 'How can a person do something like that! A father, for heaven's sake! All the kids on the island go swimming here – and he's poisoning the place with all this . . . this . . .'

'Ca-ca?' said Abbey.

'Whatever,' my mother fumed. 'The man ought to be in jail. He's a menace to the public health.'

Dad has a long list of people that he says should be locked up for one thing or another, but this was the first time I'd ever heard Mom say that about anybody.

My grandfather also was angered by what he saw, although he tried not to show it. 'Jail's too good for the lowlife who did this,' he said evenly, 'but it's a start.'

Abbey and I looked uneasily at each other. We'd seen Grandpa Bobby in action before.

'Paine, you 'member that big muttonfish I caught here?' he asked my father. 'The fifteen-pounder?'

'You bet I remember. Only it was fourteen pounds,' Dad said. 'Fourteen even.'

'Sure? Anyways, it was a helluva catch,' said Grandpa Bobby. 'That was back before they dropped fish traps all over the reefs. Back before certain creeps started dumping their crapola in the sea.'

There was a rumbly edge to his voice, like he was struggling to keep his temper under control.

Mom said, 'Don't worry, Pop. Someday Dusty Muleman will get exactly what he deserves. People like him always do.

This was her famous what-goes-around-comes-around theory. My grandfather obviously didn't buy it, although he was too polite to say so. He picked up a branch of driftwood and swept it back and forth through the stained water.

'Somebody probably oughta notify the coast guard while the tide's right,' he said.

I didn't mention the phone call I'd made earlier at the house. As if on cue, a sound like a rolling drumbeat rose from the north.

Abbey said, 'Listen, guys! You hear that?'

Thwock-a-thwock-a-thwock . . .

We all turned and looked up.

'Over there!' said Dad. He has eyes like an osprey; the rest of us couldn't see a thing.

After a while my grandfather spotted it, too, and pointed where to look. At first it was just a small fuzzy dot in the wide open blueness of the sky. But as the dot grew larger, it turned blaze orange and took on the shape of a helicopter.

The drumbeat of the rotors became a loud, high-pitched whine as the chopper circled lower. On its belly we could plainly read the words COAST GUARD. A side door rolled open, and a man in a dark jump-suit leaned out. He was wearing a white crash helmet and aiming a camera down at the water.

Taking video of our amazing fuchsia river.

We waved at the coast guard man, but he was too busy to wave back. The helicopter gradually began to move, following the colourful current of evidence all the way up the beach, all the way to the marina where the *Coral Queen* was moored. There the chopper hovered for a long, long time.

Dusty Muleman was officially busted.

Abbey whooped and Grandpa Bobby clapped and I pumped a fist in the air. We headed home feeling hopeful and happy – though Dad and Mom weren't quite happy enough to forget about me and Abbey sneaking out the night before.

'By the way, you're both grounded,' Mom informed us in the car.

I signalled for Abbey to stay cool, but she ignored me.

'Grounded for how long?' she asked indignantly.

'Indefinitely,' Dad said.

Which was better than setting an exact number of days or weeks. From experience I knew that an 'indefinite' grounding could be negotiated favourably – if only Abbey would quit whining.

'It's not fair,' my sister said. 'In fact, it really bites.'

'Watch your mouth, young lady,' Mom warned.

'But we just saved Thunder Beach! Don't we get bonus points for that?'

Grandpa Bobby said, 'Abbey, darlin', it won't be so bad. Anyway, it's probably a smart idea for you and your brother to lay low for a while.'

And he was the family expert on laying low.

I waited until we got back to the house before asking my parents to delay the starting date of our grounding. 'Just until tomorrow,' I said. 'Please?'

My father eyed me suspiciously. 'Why? You've got big plans for this afternoon?'

'I need to go thank Shelly.'

'Me too,' said Abbey, scooting to my side.

Dad left the decision to Mom, who drilled us with one of her I'm-not-kidding stares. 'You've got exactly one hour,' she said. 'Not a minute more.'

We dashed for our bikes, Abbey calling over her shoulder, 'Grandpa Bobby, you'd better be here when we get back!'

*

My mother and father honestly care about each other, but they argue about plenty of stuff. Sometimes it seems silly to me and Abbey, but other times it's really heavy. For instance, Mom was ninety-nine per cent serious about divorcing Dad if he didn't come home from jail and get his act together. I totally understood why she felt like that, and at the same time I could see the point he was trying to make by sinking the *Coral Queen*.

But even when my parents are fighting, they don't actually fight. It's only sharp words back and forth; no fists or blunt objects.

Unfortunately, some people really get carried away – as my sister and I were reminded when we showed up at Shelly's trailer.

She was sitting on the steps, gazing off into the distance. She wore black jeans, a grey Gap T-shirt, and a blue trucker's cap turned backward.

In one hand was a sweaty bottle of beer, and in the other hand was a rake. Some of the tines were snapped off, and others were bent at sharp angles. It wasn't the sort of damage caused by normal, everyday gardening.

'What's wrong?' I asked.

'Love is a strange deal, I swear,' she said. 'You wanna come in? It's a awful mess, I'll be honest.'

'We'll help you clean up,' Abbey offered.

'What kind of mess?' I asked.

'Like nothin' you ever saw before,' Shelly said. 'Think you can handle it?'

After seeing the condition of the rake, I wasn't so sure. To stall I asked her what had happened on the *Coral Queen* after I'd jumped overboard.

She laughed. 'Nobody heard a thing because the band was so loud. Everybody just kept drinkin' and gamblin'. The customers who saw you run past, they figured you belonged to one of the crew.'

'What about that nasty old lady who tried to break into the bathroom?'

'Oh, her? Free stack of chips and she was back at the blackjack table, happy as a clam,' Shelly reported. 'Speaking of bathrooms, I had to make, like, *seven* trips before I got rid of all that purple goo. Every time I'd get settled nice and cosy, somebody'd start bangin' on the door, sayin' they couldn't wait. My wrist hurts from flushin' so much.'

'But our plan worked!' Abbey piped eagerly. 'Did you hear the helicopter fly over? That was the coast guard – we saw 'em taking video of the stain in the water.'

'No kidding?' Shelly looked pleased. She stood up, spinning the rake like a cheerleader's baton.

'Did Dusty say anything after the casino closed?' I asked.

'Naw, he was a total basket case,' Shelly said. 'There was some big fight on the docks, and Luno got his butt seriously whipped, is what I heard. One of the bouncers drove him to the hospital and then the cops showed up, asking what happened, but by then Dusty'd already split. The crew didn't know any different, so they waited until all the people were gone and pumped the holding tank straight into the basin, same as usual.'

I told Shelly she'd done a great job. 'Thanks for emptying that liquor crate so I had a place to hide, and for sneaking me into the ladies' head, and most of all for risking your neck to help us out . . .'

'Yeah, you did awesome,' said Abbey. 'But what about Dusty's secret spy at the coast guard station? How'd you fix it so he wasn't around this morning when Noah called in about the *Coral Queen*?'

Shelly propped the rake on one shoulder, like a rifle. 'Come on in,' she said to us. 'But, like I said, it's not a pretty picture.'

She wasn't kidding. Inside the trailer it looked like a small bomb had exploded – broken lamps, overturned furniture, dents and holes in the fake-wood panelling.

Two rumpled men lay facedown – one on the gross shag carpet, one on the gross mouldy sofa. We couldn't see their faces, so it was hard to tell if they were dead or alive. The one on the floor was sopping wet and striped green with slime from the aquarium, which lay on its side, empty and cracked.

Shelly used the rake handle to poke at the unconscious man on the sofa. 'You asked about Mr Billy Babcock? Well, here he is.'

Billy Babcock made a low snuffling sound, but he didn't move.

'What'd you do to him?' Abbey asked.

'Nothin' he didn't want done,' Shelly replied with a snort. 'He spent about two hours yakkin' at my bar last night. I figured the only way to guarantee that he wouldn't be at work this morning was to bring him home with me and—'

'We get the idea,' I cut in, not wanting Abbey to hear the R-rated details.

'That's cool, Noah, watchin' out for your little sister,' Shelly said, 'but don't worry – I was a perfect lady. I invited Billy over for one of my high-octane cocktails, maybe two. All we did was hold hands on the couch until he got tired of tellin' me how gorgeous and wonderful I was. Then he keeled over and went nighty-night.'

'So who's the other guy?' I pointed at the soggy heap on the floor.

'You don't recognize him?' Shelly chuckled again. Using the business end of the rake, she snagged the man's ooze-covered shirt and rolled him onto his back. When I saw that pasty sunken face, I was completely blown away.

'Well? Who is it?' my sister asked impatiently.

'That's Lice Peeking,' I said.

'In person!' Shelly unhooked the rake from his shirt. 'I told you, love's a strange deal.'

'Is he alive?' Abbey asked.

'More or less,' Shelly replied. 'You guys want a Coke?'

We sat at the dinette and listened to her story. It was a good one.

After my father had gone to jail and started spouting off about the *Coral Queen*, Dusty Muleman had gotten nervous. He'd made a list of everyone besides Dad who knew the truth about the pollution scam, and he had sent Luno to warn each person to keep quiet – or else. The goon hadn't murdered Lice Peeking, as Shelly had thought, but he had scared the bodily fluids out of him.

When Luno had shown up at the trailer, Lice naturally assumed that Dusty had found out about his secret deal with Dad – the bonefish skiff in exchange for Lice's testimony. So as soon as Luno left, Lice swiped Shelly's Jeep and drove full speed for the mainland. True to form, he forgot to fill the gas tank.

When it was empty, he simply parked the truck and took off on foot.

'But what about the bloodstains on the seats?' I asked.

Shelly shook her head sheepishly. 'Ketchup,' she said. 'The slob was pigging out on Big Macs and fries for forty miles.'

Abbey said, 'Why'd he come back? Did he run out of money or something?'

'You're a very sharp young lady. Yeah, he ran out of money,' Shelly said, 'but that's not why he came back to the Keys. See, he missed me. Deep down in his heart, he truly did.'

I cringed when my sister asked, 'How can you possibly believe that?'

'Because the man knew for a fact what would happen if I ever laid eyes on him again. He knew I'd whup him like the sorry, no-good jackass he is – yet he came back anyway! If that ain't true love, it's close enough for me,' said Shelly.

The timing of Lice Peeking's return couldn't have been worse. It was past three in the morning when he'd flung open the trailer door, only to find his cherished Shelly reading an astrology magazine on the couch – with a snoozing Billy Babcock stretched out beside her. In a jealous fit Lice Peeking had jumped on Billy, kicking and punching and scratching.

That was when Shelly had run to the toolshed.

Being whacked with a rake seemed to work miracles on Lice Peeking's attitude – he'd dropped to one knee, told Shelly he adored her, and blubbered he was sorry for all the rotten deeds he'd ever done.

'Even promised to pay back the hundred and eighty-six dollars he took, plus the towing charges for the Jeep,' Shelly said. 'I'll never see a nickel, for sure, but still it was a nice sentiment. I told Lice to quit beggin' and get off the floor, and that's when the fool grabbed the aquarium stand to pull himself up. Whole tank tipped over on top of him, all fifty gallons, and off to dreamland he went.'

It wouldn't have been a huge shock to learn that Shelly had purposely dumped the grungy aquarium on Lice Peeking, but I took her word that it was an accident. Anything was possible.

'What about the fish?' Abbey asked worriedly.

'There was only one left, the loneliest, most pitiful guppy you ever saw. I put him in the bathtub,' Shelly said.

'And him?' I nodded toward Billy Babcock.

'Slept through all the fun, believe it or not.' Shelly nudged him again with the rake handle. 'Once he wakes up, I'll clue him in on what happened. Otherwise he'll be curious about all those fresh bruises and fingernail marks.'

I went over to take a close look at Lice Peeking. The toppling aquarium had left a plum-sized knot on his forehead. His T-shirt showed several rows of small bloody holes where Shelly's rake had dug in, but he seemed to be feeling no pain. He snored peacefully, blowing snot bubbles from his nose.

Abbey said to Shelly, 'What a loser! I can't believe you're taking him back.'

'It's none of your business, princess, but let's say it was. Let's say you were my mother and you were upset about me hangin' out with this lame excuse for a boyfriend. I'd tell you that I'm a big girl with my eyes wide open. Made a few dumb mistakes of my own, but I was always grateful for a second chance. And trust me,' Shelly said, 'that's all Lice Peeking is gettin' – one more chance. Look here, he even went and bought me some new earrings.'

Shelly pulled back her thick hair to reveal five small, shiny hoops in her left ear. Abbey admitted they looked cool.

'Yeah, they do.' Shelly turned to me. 'Noah, what does your daddy think is gonna happen to Dusty Muleman?'

'He says the coast guard will probably shut down the *Coral Queen* right away. He says they won't throw Dusty in jail, but they could make him pay out a fortune in fines.'

'But if the boat's out of business, then you're out of a job,' Abbey said to Shelly. 'What are you going to do?'

'Don't worry about me, princess. Being a bartender in the Keys is like being a roofer in hurricane season. You're never out of work for long.'

The trailer was such a disaster that sweeping and mopping seemed like a waste of energy; it should have been towed straight to the county dump. But it was Shelly's only home, so I said, 'We're going to help you fix up this place.'

'You'll do no such thing.' She steered us toward the door. 'I got all the help I need, these two turkeys ever wake up.'

She gave each of us a quick hug, then closed the door.

Abbey checked her watch and announced that we had exactly eleven minutes to get home or else we'd be grounded until the next century. We took off down the old road as fast we could.

Ahead I spotted two familiar figures, one running and the other pedalling a beach cruiser beside him. Abbey noticed them, too.

'Noah, don't stop,' she said through clenched teeth. 'No matter what.'

And I wouldn't have stopped, either, if only Jasper Jr hadn't called me an exceptionally insulting name as we flew past. Next thing I knew, I felt myself hit the brakes. It was pure reflex. After all that had happened, I just couldn't pass up the opportunity to brighten Jasper Jr's day.

'Are you completely whacked?' Abbey whispered.

'Keep going,' I told her firmly. 'I'm not kidding.'

She knew it, too. She kept riding.

I spun the bike around and waited. Jasper Jr was on the beach cruiser, and Bull was jogging to keep up – beet-faced and sweating buckets.

'Where you guys going?' I asked pleasantly. 'To the marina maybe? To have a chat with the coast guard?'

Jasper Jr hopped off the bike and let it fall. I could see that he was boiling mad. He stalked up to me and grabbed my handlebars and wrenched them back and forth, trying to knock me off.

Somehow I kept my balance, and I also kept the smile on my face. It was driving him nuts.

'OK, dorkbrain, let's do it!' Jasper Jr snarled. 'You and me! Right now!'

'Jasper, don't start nothin',' Bull said, bending over to catch his breath.

Very calmly I climbed off my bicycle and put down the kickstand. Then I stepped up to Jasper Jr and got right in his face. When he reached up to shove me, I knocked his arms away. He seemed totally amazed.

I couldn't stop smiling. Being afraid of those two boneheads seemed so ridiculous, I'd rather have taken another punch in the eye than run away.

'Come on, dude,' Bull said to Jasper Jr. 'Let's go.'

'Oh no you don't. Not yet,' I said. 'He still owes me an apology. In fact, he owes me two, after what he just called me.'

'You're so dead!' Jasper Jr snapped. '*So dead!*'

The way he was moving his ratlike mouth, I knew he was working up another loogie to spit on me. I reached under my shirt and pulled out the chain that was hanging from my neck.

The ancient gold coin dangled back and forth, glinting in the sunlight. From the bug-eyed way that Jasper Jr and Bull were staring, I knew they recognized the coin as the one that Grandpa Bobby was wearing that day in the woods.

Bull took a shaky half step backward. Jasper Jr stood there gnawing on his lower lip, which I took as a sign of possible brain activity. Neither of them wanted to tangle with that crazy old pirate again.

'I'm still waiting for my apologies,' I said.

Bull poked Jasper Jr. 'Get it over with, dude.' Then Bull picked up the beach cruiser, hopped on, and pedalled away.

Jasper Jr shifted uneasily as he watched his friend ride off. Now it was just me and him. I'd like to think he would've been nervous even if I hadn't shown him the coin, but probably not.

He turned his knobby walnut head and hawked on the pavement. 'I'm sorry, Underwood,' he mumbled, barely loud enough for me to hear.

'One down,' I said, 'and one more to go.'

It was obviously painful, but Jasper Jr forced himself to say it again. 'I'm sorry, OK? *S-o-r-y.*'

'Close enough.' I stepped back and waved him down the road.

Jasper Jr gave me one of his trademark sneers and took off running.

'Have a nice day,' I called, though I knew it probably wouldn't turn out that way for the Muleman family.

NINETEEN

Naturally the story was huge in the *Island Examiner*. The headline blared:

CASINO BOAT BUSTED IN POLLUTION PROBE

Miles Umlatt wrote the article, which explained that the flushed waste was traced easily to the *Coral Queen* because the crud contained 'a highly visible, inky-coloured substance'. The front page of the newspaper featured an aerial photograph of our incriminating fuchsia stain. Not to brag, but it *was* impressive.

As my father had predicted, the coast guard shut down the gambling boat right away. Dusty Muleman was not available for comment.

Miles Umlatt and a couple of other reporters called our house and left messages. They all wanted to interview Dad, now that his accusations against Dusty had been proven true.

The old Paine Underwood would have eagerly picked up the phone and ranted, but the new Paine

Underwood took Donna Underwood's advice and let it ring off the hook.

My father didn't need to say anything to the newspaper because everyone in town knew the truth by now. They knew he was right about Dusty after all.

The following morning Grandpa Bobby borrowed Dad's pickup and drove to Miami Beach to surprise Uncle Del and Aunt Sandy. He said they were really happy to see him alive, but after a while they started acting kind of nervous and weird. They were probably freaking out, trying to think of a way to explain how they'd spent all that money my grandfather had left in the bank box.

A day later he returned to the Keys and stayed with us for a week – one of the neatest times of my life. Even Abbey got jazzed. Every night we'd stay up late, listening to his Caribbean adventures. In the daytime we went snorkelling or crabbing or wakeboarding behind the skiff. One afternoon we took a metal detector to the sandbar where all the drunk tourists from Miami hang out, and we found thirteen dollars in change, four rings, two bracelets, a brand new Swiss army knife, and somebody's gold molar.

Suddenly, over breakfast one morning, Grandpa Bobby announced he was leaving.

'Where?' I asked.

Dad answered for him. 'Back to South America.'

Grandpa Bobby nodded. 'You're not gonna come huntin' for me, are you, Paine? I want a promise.'

'You've got it,' my father said, not happily.

Grandpa Bobby hitched a silvery eyebrow at my mother. 'Donna, I'm countin' on you to keep this hot-headed husband of yours from runnin' off the rails.'

Mom told Grandpa Bobby not to worry. 'We'll miss you, Pop,' she said.

'But why are you leaving?' Abbey blurted. 'Why won't you stay here with us?'

'It's tempting, tiger, it truly is,' my grandfather said, 'but don't forget, the US government thinks I'm dead. When the time's right, I'll be proud to march into the American embassy and stamp my fingerprint on a piece of paper and clear up all the confusion. But for now it's useful that certain folks don't know I'm alive. I've got some important business to clear up, before I can come home for good.'

My sister bolted from the table, but she didn't get far. Grandpa Bobby snagged her as she dashed by and pulled her into his arms. He used his faded bandanna to dry her cheeks.

'What if something bad happens?' Abbey cried. 'I don't want you to die for real.'

'But I can't *live* for real until I finish this thing,' he said. 'Please try to understand.'

He fished something out of his pocket. 'These are

for you, Abbey. It's only fair, since your brother got the queen's coin.'

Abbey's eyes nearly popped out of her head. 'Whoa,' she said under her breath.

We all leaned in for a close look at the two green earrings. The stones were small but the colour was brilliant, like reef water.

'Emeralds,' Grandpa Bobby said.

Mom was dazzled, too. 'I won't ask where you got them,' she said.

'Oh, probably another "poker game",' Dad remarked.

'Don't worry, I earned 'em fair and square,' said Grandpa Bobby. 'I've been carrying 'em around for years, hopin' to meet just the right girl. Now I have.'

He dropped the emerald studs into Abbey's palm and said, 'Those little greenies are worth more than diamonds.'

'They're worth even more than *that*,' said Abbey, 'to me.'

I'd never seen my sister so excited. After Mom helped her put on the earrings, she ran to check herself out in the hall mirror.

Grandpa Bobby said, 'Abbey, you're as lovely as your grandmother was. I only wish you could've known her.' He looked at my father. 'And, son, I wish . . .'

He didn't finish the sentence. Slowly he got up and went out the back door. Through the window we could see him sag against the trunk of our big mahogany tree. He was rubbing his eyes.

'Do you still remember her?' I asked my father.

'Like it was yesterday, Noah.'

Then he went outside and put an arm around the old pirate's shoulders.

Sometimes my parents make me slightly crazed, but the thought of losing either one of them is so unreal that I can't imagine it. I can't even *try* to imagine it.

All these years, I never considered the possibility that my father – my well-meaning but occasionally whacked-out father – might be walking around with a broken heart, carrying a pain too awful to talk about.

I mean, his mom died when he was a kid. *Died.*

How could anyone be the same afterward? How could there not be a huge sad hole in your life?

And how could it not get worse when somebody calls up to say that your father's gone, too? The father you idolized – dead and buried in some faraway jungle.

So maybe Dad filled up all that emptiness another way. Whenever he saw something bad or wrong, he'd do just about anything to make it right, no matter how reckless or foolish. It's possible he couldn't help himself.

I think Mom understood. I think that's why she's been so patient through the rough times.

And maybe Dad will be better, now that he knows Grandpa Bobby is really alive. It's something to hope for anyway.

On the afternoon before he left, my grandfather knocked on my bedroom door and said he wanted to go fishing. We grabbed a couple of spinning rods and headed off to Thunder Beach.

The water was crystal clear, and we waded up to our knees. Scads of minnows flashed like chrome spangles in the shallows, and right away we spooked a snaggle-toothed barracuda that had been hanging motionless near a coral head.

Grandpa Bobby started casting a small yellow bucktail, hopping it through the grassy patches where the snappers hang out.

'How are you going back?' I asked.

'Same way I got here. There's a freighter leaving Key West for Aruba tomorrow,' he said. 'From there I'll hitch a ride on a banana boat.'

'You sure about this?'

Grandpa Bobby said, 'Oh, I'll be fine. Your mom even packed me a suitcase.'

'Not the plaid one?' I asked.

'Yeah. What's so funny?'

'That's the one she takes out whenever she's thinking about dumping Dad.'

'Well, I guess that's not in the game plan any more.' My grandfather tucked the butt of the fishing rod under one arm and took out another old photograph to show me.

'There she is,' he said proudly.

It was a picture of the *Amanda Rose*. She was a classic, too.

'That was taken in Cat Cay,' he said. 'Summer before you were born.'

'Wow.'

'She's forty-six feet. Twin diesels, eight hundred horses.'

The gleaming sport-fisherman was tied stern-first to a wooden dock, where a monster blue marlin hung glassy-eyed from a tall pole. In the picture Grandpa Bobby's curly hair was so long, it looked like a blond Afro. He was poised on the teakwood transom, raising a beer in a toast to the great fish.

'The dirtbags who hijacked my *Amanda Rose*, they've repainted the hull and changed her name. But that won't fly,' he said confidently, 'because I'll recognize her, no matter what.'

'But what if you can't find her?' I asked.

'Oh, I most definitely will, Noah. You can bet the

damn ranch on that.' He didn't take his eyes off the photograph. 'I built her myself. Started shortly after your grandmother passed on. It was this boat that carried me through those terrible times. That, and raising your daddy and his brother and sister.'

He folded up the snapshot and went back to fishing.

'All this might be tough for you to understand,' he said quietly.

'Not at all.'

'Ten years is ridiculous, Noah. Ten years without so much as a postcard. I'm lucky your father forgave me.'

'I wish I could've seen his face the night you showed up,' I said.

Grandpa Bobby laughed. 'Know what he did? He jumped from the truck and snatched me up and swung me round in circles like a doll – same as I did to him when he was a little shrimp! He's got some serious muscle on his bones, your old man does. Hey, what's this? Finally somebody got hungry.'

He jerked up on the rod and reeled in a small blue runner, which he tossed back. He caught another one on the very next cast.

'Hey, aren't you gonna fish?' he asked me.

'Sure.' I threw my bucktail into the deeper water and started bouncing it along the bottom.

'How come you're so quiet?' he said.

The truth was, I felt as bummed out as Abbey – I didn't want Grandpa Bobby to go away again. At the same time I didn't want to make him feel guilty by saying so.

He said, 'You don't believe I'll ever be back, do you?'

'I'm worried, that's all.' It was impossible not to worry. The knife scar on his cheek was a pretty strong clue that the men my grandfather was chasing were not model citizens.

'Whatever else they say about me, champ, I do keep my promises.'

'Yeah, but—'

'Hey, are you snagged on a rock?'

'No, I don't think so.'

It was a fish. As soon as I set the hook, it smoked thirty yards of line off the spool. Grandpa Bobby whistled.

'Probably just a big jack,' I said.

'Wanna bet?'

The fish fought hard, dogging back and forth across the flats. It made several more zippy runs – one between my ankles – before I was able to steer it to the beach.

My grandfather was right. It wasn't a jack. It was a fat pink snapper. Triumphantly he pointed at the black telltale spot on its side. 'That's a muttonfish, Noah!'

'Sweet,' I said. It was the best snapper I'd ever caught. 'How big do you think it is?'

He smiled. 'How big do you want it to be?'

'Just the truth,' I told him.

'The truth? Six pounds,' he said, 'but that's still one helluva catch on a bucktail jig from a shoreline.'

I held the fish still while Grandpa Bobby unhooked it. You have to be super careful because snappers can bite through a human finger, no problem.

'Noah, you hungry? I'm not.'

'Me neither.'

'Good,' said Grandpa Bobby.

He nudged the fish back into the water. It kicked its tail and tore off.

'Must be some kind of mystic Underwood karma,' he said. 'This looks like the very same spot where I caught that nice mutton with your daddy, gotta be twenty-five, thirty years ago.'

'How big was yours again?' I knew it was either fourteen or fifteen pounds, depending on who was telling the story. I was curious to hear which version Grandpa Bobby was in the mood for.

He said, 'Your daddy recalls it as fourteen on the button, and his memory's likely better than mine.'

'Still a beast.'

'Yeah, but you got your whole life to catch one bigger. You'll do it, too, there's no doubt in my mind.'

'Because of the karma?'

'Somethin' like that,' he said. 'You done fishin'?'

'I think so.'

'Me too.'

We put down our rods and sat on the sand. With the change of tide a breeze had kicked up, blowing in from the direction of the lighthouse. We could see two tankers and a cruise ship, all northbound in the Gulf Stream.

Another loggerhead turtle surfaced in the chop off the beach. It was twice as big and crusty as the one I'd seen with Abbey and Shelly. This time, though, I didn't need to jump in and scare it away.

Today the water looked perfect, the way it was a million years ago, before people started using the ocean as a latrine. Today it was awesomely pure and bright, and totally safe for an old loggerhead to browse the grassy flats. Chow down. Chill out. Take a snooze.

'Don't be surprised,' Grandpa Bobby said, 'if one sunny day you're swimmin' here at the beach – or maybe just takin' a stroll with some girl – when a certain magnificent forty-six-footer comes haulin' ass over that pearly blue horizon, yours truly up in the tuna tower.'

The thing was, I could picture the moment perfectly in my mind. All I had to do was close my eyes, and there was Robert Lee Underwood streaking across the waves in the *Amanda Rose*.

'Now, Noah, I'm not tellin' you to sit around and wait for me. That would be downright pathetic.' He laughed and chucked my arm. 'All I'm sayin' is, don't be surprised when the day comes.'

'I won't,' I said. 'Not even a little bit.'

TWENTY

The summer ended quietly, and that was fine with me. Rado came back from Colorado with an infected cactus needle in his chin, and Thom came back from North Carolina with spider bites in both armpits. I didn't have any gross wounds to show off, but I had the story of Operation Royal Flush to tell, which made both my friends wish they'd been here to help.

A few days after school started, a cheque for a thousand dollars arrived in the mail at our house. The cheque was made out to my father, who thought it was a mistake. It wasn't.

The Florida Keys are a national marine sanctuary, which means that the islands are supposedly protected by special laws against pollution, poaching, and other man-made damage. The sanctuary programme offers cash rewards to anybody who calls in tips about serious environmental crimes.

Dad's reward was one thousand dollars.

'But I wasn't the one who phoned in about the

gambling boat,' he told a man at the sanctuary office.

'Then it was somebody using your name and phone number,' the man said. 'If I were you, Mr Underwood, I'd keep the money and forget about it.'

I purposely hadn't told my father that it was me who called the coast guard on Dusty Muleman the morning after we'd flushed the dye. If Dad had known, he would have insisted that me and Abbey keep the reward.

We figured he could use the money to cover some of the damage caused to the casino boat when he sunk it. Dad still had to repay Dusty, even though Dusty had been busted.

So I felt pretty good seeing that cheque on the kitchen counter. It was a thousand bucks that didn't have to come out of my father's pocket.

Before long my sister and I were so caught up with school that neither of us thought much about the *Coral Queen*, or about what might happen to Dusty Muleman. We just assumed that the government would put him out of business – after all, he'd been caught cold, dumping hundreds of gallons of poop into protected state waters. It was one of the worst cases ever documented in Monroe County, according to the *Island Examiner*.

Meanwhile, something good was in the works. A bunch of the other fishing guides had written to the coast guard, saying Dad ought to be given one more chance with his captain's licence. And to almost everyone's surprise, the coast guard agreed – but only if Dad finished his anger-control therapy and got a letter saying he was all better.

It was sweet news for our family. Although my father was making good money at Tropical Rescue, his patience for numskull behaviour was running out. Almost every night he'd tell us a new horror story about some macho moron driving a go-fast boat aground and gouging a hundred-yard scar across the turtle grass.

I had a feeling it was only a matter of time before Dad towed one of those knuckleheads somewhere other than back to the dock; somewhere far away, where it would be a long, hot, miserable wait until anybody found them.

So we were really amped to know that Dad would soon be back in his skiff, guiding for bonefish and tarpon and snook. Almost overnight he seemed happy again, nearly as happy as when Grandpa Bobby had been here. Mom promised to take everybody out for stone crabs to celebrate when the big day arrived.

But less than a month before the coast guard was due to return Dad's licence, more trouble kicked up. I came home from school and found a large splintered hole in the centre of our front door. There was another hole in the kitchen door, and still another in the door of the hallway bathroom.

It was impossible not to notice that each of the holes was about the same size as my father's fist.

Mom looked frazzled when she came down the hall.

'What happened?' I asked.

She shook her head sombrely. 'Your dad got some bad news.'

My knees started to buckle – I was afraid something terrible had happened to Grandpa Bobby.

'It's about Dusty Muleman,' my mother said. 'His lawyers worked out some sweetheart deal with the government. He's reopening the *Coral Queen* tonight, throwing a big party for the whole town . . .'

I should've been ticked off, too, but at that moment I was more worried about Dad.

'Mom, tell me he didn't use his bare hands on the doors.'

'Oh yes, indeed.'

Just thinking about it was painful. I said, 'Who's teaching those anger-control classes – Mike Tyson?'

'It's certainly a setback,' my mother said unhappily. 'They've been counselling your dad to get rid of negative energy the moment it enters his head. Somehow I don't think this is what they had in mind.'

'How bad is it?'

Mom motioned toward their bedroom. 'He's resting quietly now,' she said. 'Why don't you go have a talk with him? I've got to pick up your sister from her piano lesson.'

Dad was lying down, watching cheesy old music videos on VH1. Each of his hands was covered by a plaster cast, and each cast was as large as a honey-dew melon.

He looked up with an embarrassed smile. 'Could be worse,' he said.

'That's true. At least you're not in jail this time,' I said.

'And it was only doors that got smashed. Those I can fix myself.'

I sat on the edge of the bed, trying not to stare. I still couldn't believe what he'd done to himself. 'You really feel like you're improving?' I asked.

My father nodded confidently. 'I think the counselling has helped, Noah, I honestly do.'

Like I said, sometimes he's on his own weird little planet.

A video came on with a chubby guy dressed up like a woman, lipstick and all. Dad hoisted one of his casts and dropped it on the remote control. The TV screen went blank.

'Be glad you weren't around in the eighties,' he

said. 'The worst music and the worst hair in the history of the human race – that's no lie.'

'Mom's pretty upset,' I told him.

'I've been a disappointment to her. I realize that.' Dad pulled himself upright and gazed out the window and didn't say anything for a while.

'She'll be all right,' I said, to break the silence.

'Yeah, she's amazing. Rock solid.'

He turned to face me and cleared his throat a couple of times. 'Noah, I'm going to tell you how things work in the real world. It might make you mad or sick to your stomach, whatever – but I want you to listen closely. OK?'

I said sure – and braced for one of his rants.

'You know how much Dusty Muleman got fined for dumping his holding tank? For fouling nature with that awful crap? Guess what his punishment was!' My father was trembling with fury. 'Ten thousand lousy dollars! Ten grand – that's what he makes in *one stinking night* off that casino operation. It's a joke, son. It's chump change to a rich maggot like that!'

'Dad, take it easy—'

'No, you need to hear this. You need to know.' He hunched forward, eyes blazing. 'Last year a few young hotshots from the federal prosecutor's office in Miami drove down here for a private bachelor party on the

Coral Queen. You know what a bachelor party is, right?'

'No, but I'll be glad to do some research.' I was trying to lighten the mood. 'Yes, Dad, I know what a bachelor party is.'

'Don't be a smartass, son. Just listen and learn. The party gets a little out of control, OK? On the boat there are some . . . well, let's be nice and call them "dancers". Exotic-type dancers—'

'I get the idea, Dad.'

'Anyway, Dusty takes out a camera and he snaps some pictures. Now, these aren't the sort of pictures that a person would necessarily want to frame and hang on the living-room wall—'

'Hold on,' I said. 'You're telling me that Dusty Muleman blackmailed the government's lawyers?'

'Let's say he didn't hesitate to tell their boss what happened that night – and what was on that roll of film,' Dad said, 'which I'm sure Dusty has locked away in a vault somewhere. Anyway, all of a sudden the feds are looking to cut a deal and close the case.'

'For a fine of ten thousand bucks.'

'It would've been even less, if it weren't for Lice Peeking,' my father said. 'He showed up one day at the coast guard station and gave a secret statement, testifying about what he saw when he used to work on the casino boat. He swore that Dusty ordered the crew to flush the holding tank whenever it got full, as long as nobody was around to see.'

I smiled to myself. That was pure Shelly – forcing Lice Peeking to step up and tell what he knew. It was obviously part of the price he had to pay if he wanted to be her boyfriend again.

'So Dusty agreed to cough up the ten grand,' Dad went on, 'and he promised never, ever again to flush into the basin.'

'And they believed him? After all this?' I said. It was incredible.

'Oh, and dig this. To show how much he cares about the ocean, he offers to throw a big fund-raising benefit for the Save the Reef Foundation on the *Coral Queen*.' Dad chuckled bitterly. 'It would be funny if only it were a movie and not real life.'

Now I understood why he'd slugged the doors. It was the surest way to stop himself from doing the same thing to Dusty Muleman.

'What happened to Luno?' I asked.

'He's back in Morocco, probably living the high life,' my father said. 'Dusty paid him off and put him on a jet, in case the feds went looking for him.'

'How'd you find this stuff out?'

'Shelly told me,' he said. 'She's slick. Dusty still hasn't got a clue that she was in on your sting.'

Dad was thirsty, so I brought him some water and

tipped the glass to his lips. He said that six of his ten knuckles had been fractured and that the doctors weren't sure when the casts could come off.

'Until then, I guess I'm out of action,' he said dejectedly, 'unless I learn how to steer a boat with my feet.'

'But you're still getting back your captain's licence, right?'

'Absolutely, Noah. There's no law against punching out your own house.'

We heard Mom's car rolling into the driveway.

'Why don't you let me be the one to tell Abbey all this,' I suggested.

'Good idea,' Dad said, 'but be sure to leave out the part about the dancers.'

That night I was jolted awake by wailing sirens, one after another. I figured there was a bad wreck somewhere on the highway. The clock by my bed said 4:20.

With all the noise, it took me a while to go back to sleep. The next thing I recall, it was daylight and Abbey was shaking me by the shoulders.

'Get up, Noah, hurry!' she whispered. 'The cops are here to arrest Dad!'

I jumped into a pair of jeans and ran to the living room. Abbey was a half step behind me.

My father was still in his pyjamas, and sitting in his favourite armchair. On each side of him stood a uniformed sheriff's deputy. I recognized one of them as the jowly guy from the jailhouse.

Standing in front of Dad was a young, barrel-chested man wearing a shiny blue suit. The man was jotting in a notebook, except he wasn't a newspaper reporter. He was a detective.

'This is Lieutenant Shucker,' said my mother.

Abbey and I nodded hello. We were real nervous, though not as nervous as Dad. Mom was pouring coffee into his mouth as fast as he could slurp it down.

'Mr Underwood, what happened to your hands?' Lieutenant Shucker asked. 'You didn't happen to burn them, did you?'

'No, I didn't burn 'em. I broke 'em,' my father said. 'Donna, show him the door.'

'I'm not going anywhere,' the detective said curtly.

'No, I mean show him the *holes* in the doors,' Dad explained.

Lieutenant Shucker examined the damage, but he didn't seem impressed.

'Where were you this morning,' he asked my dad, 'between three a.m. and four a.m.?'

'He's been right here with us,' my mother interjected.

'That's right,' I said. 'Dad was home all night.'

'How do you know that for sure?' the detective asked snidely.

Abbey looked as if she wanted to bite him. 'Geez, mister, check out his hands!' she said. 'He can't pick his own nose, much less drive a car!'

The two deputies began to snicker, then caught themselves. Mom's jaw tightened. 'Abbey, that'll be enough from you.'

Dad tried to act indignant by folding his arms, but the casts were too bulky. 'Officers, what's this all about?' he demanded.

'Mr Underwood, you have the right to remain silent,' Lieutenant Shucker said. 'You also have the right to an attorney—'

'Wait a minute! Hold on!' I burst out. 'You're arresting him?'

'Not right this minute,' the detective said, 'but we've got lots more questions. He's definitely our prime suspect in this crime.'

'What crime?' Abbey and I exclaimed in unison.

'Yeah, what crime?' asked my father.

'Burning down the *Coral Queen*,' Lieutenant Shucker replied. 'It's called arson.'

TWENTY-ONE

The detective wouldn't tell us anything more, but Shelly filled us in by phone later. It was a wild story.

Dusty Muleman had invited all the local big shots and politicians to the grand reopening of the casino boat. They all showed up, too, since Shelly was pouring free drinks. There were fireworks, a lobster buffet, and calypso music from the steel-drum band. The party rocked on until two in the morning. Afterward it took Shelly forty-five minutes to clean up the bar, and she was one of the last to leave the boat.

The first explosion took place shortly after three a.m., and within half an hour the *Coral Queen* was on fire from bow to stern. The new watchman, Luno's replacement, nearly fried when a falling cinder ignited the ticket shed, where he was phoning for help. The watchman made a frantic attempt to douse the flames with a dock hose, then ran from the marina.

By the time the fire engines got there, the gambling boat was a floating torch. By the time Dusty Muleman got there, it had burned to the water line – seventy-three feet of smouldering ash and melted poker chips. Naturally, he believed that my father was the culprit. Knowing what Dad thought of Dusty, the sheriff didn't need much convincing.

Even Abbey felt the circumstances were suspicious.

'You think he might've had something to do with this?' she asked me in private. 'Maybe he paid somebody to go burn the boat.'

'Paid them with what?'

'How about with the thousand bucks he got from the sanctuary?'

'No way, Abbey,' I said. 'Absolutely impossible.'

But she'd gotten me worried. What if Dad *had* flipped out again? Blown another gasket. Flown off the handle.

So when we were alone, I asked him.

'I won't tell a soul if you were involved,' I said. It was a promise I wasn't sure I could keep.

'Noah, it wasn't me. I swear on a stack of Bibles.' He solemnly raised his right arm, cast and all. He was so intense that it startled me.

'I had nothing to do with torching the *Coral Queen*,' he said. 'Please believe me – and please tell Abbey to believe me, too.'

And, in the end, we did.

Because my father had never lied to us about something serious. Whenever he screwed up, he admitted it right away. He always took the blame, the responsibility – and the punishment. Why would he change now?

Mr Shine, our lawyer, was at the house when the detective and two deputies returned that afternoon with a search warrant. They snooped around for a long time, but they couldn't find anything that connected Dad to the boat arson.

Lieutenant Shucker was visibly disappointed. 'I ought to lock you up anyhow,' he said to Dad. 'It's crystal clear what happened – you had the motive, you had the opportunity . . .'

'Without evidence you've got no case,' said Mr Shine, looking less mopy than usual. 'I would kindly advise you to stop bothering my client.'

'Evidence?' the detective scoffed. 'You want evidence? Just look at the brand-new casts on his hands – obviously he burned himself while he was lighting the fire.'

Dad angrily clacked his plaster paws together. 'What a load of bull!'

'We'll see about that. I'll be back tomorrow with another warrant, Mr Underwood, and a doctor to saw off those casts. If your fingers are barbecued, you're goin' straight to the slammer.'

'But what about the fist holes in our doors?' Abbey

protested. 'That proves he's telling the truth.'

'Nice try,' Lieutenant Shucker said sarcastically, 'but you could do the same thing with a tyre iron.' Then he stood up to leave.

My mother had been sitting on the sofa, not saying a word. I figured she was just depressed, thinking about Dad returning to jail and how he might never get his captain's licence and how our quiet, semi-normal life was a total mess again. That's what *I* was thinking anyway.

But it turned out that Mom wasn't depressed at all. She was merely waiting for the right moment to drop a little stink bomb on the snotty detective.

'Here, Lieutenant,' she said pleasantly, 'you might want to take a look at this.'

She handed a computerized printout to Lieutenant Shucker, who studied it suspiciously.

'It's the bill from the emergency room,' Mom said.

'Yeah, Mrs Underwood, I can read.'

'From when my husband was admitted for severe injuries to both his hands.'

The detective frowned impatiently. 'So? What's your point?'

My mother is truly awesome in situations like that. Nothing fazes her. She stood beside Lieutenant Shucker and calmly pointed to a line of type on the computer receipt.

'He was treated for fractures, not burns. It says so right here, Lieutenant.' Mom smiled. 'That's my first point.'

The detective grunted.

'My second point,' Mom went on, 'concerns the precise time my husband arrived at the hospital. See? It was eleven thirty-three in the morning. *Yesterday* morning, Lieutenant.'

'Oh.'

'Approximately sixteen hours *before* Mr Muleman's boat was set on fire.'

'Yeah, I can do the math,' the detective grumbled.

'Which means my husband couldn't possibly have been the arsonist,' Mom said, 'unless you'd care to demonstrate how a person with all ten fingers sealed in hard plaster would go about striking a match.'

Lieutenant Shucker's big round chest seemed to deflate. Mom led him to the front door, the two deputies skulking close behind. 'Goodbye now,' she called after them, 'and good luck solving your case.'

We waited at the window until they drove away. Then Abbey started whooping, and we all slapped high fives – me, my sister, Mom, Mr Shine, even Dad with his lumpy five-pound casts.

'Donna, that was amazing,' he said. 'Truly amazing.'

'Better than amazing!' Abbey crowed. 'It was outrageous!'

'No, incredible!' I hollered. 'Amazingly, outra-
geously incredible!'

Mom blushed. 'We'll see,' she said. 'We'll just have
to wait and see.'

But Lieutenant Shucker never came back.

And later, when we learned who actually burned
down the *Coral Queen*, we congratulated my mother
all over again. Dusty Muleman had gotten exactly
what he'd deserved, just as she had predicted.

Luckily, Dad's anger-control counsellor took pity on
him and didn't mention his broken hands in her letter
to the judge. Instead, the counsellor stated that Mr
Paine Underwood had made 'significant though sometimes painful progress' in managing his temper, and
that he presented 'no immediate threat to himself, his
family, or the innocent public'.

Whether he's still a threat to innocent doors remains
to be seen.

By coincidence the coast guard sent Dad his captain's licence on the same day that the fire investigators released their findings about the *Coral Queen*.

The story took up the entire front page of the
Island Examiner, including photographs of Dusty
Muleman and the burned boat. There was no photo
of Jasper Jr, which was a shame since he was the star
of the arson report.

Dusty's first mistake had been allowing Jasper Jr and Bull to hang out aboard the *Coral Queen* on the night of the grand reopening. Dusty's second mistake had been losing track of those two nitwits while he celebrated.

By the time the party had ended, Dusty wasn't thinking too clearly. He staggered from the boat, assuming that his son had already gone home.

He was wrong. Jasper Jr and Bull had decided to throw a party of their own in one of the storage holds. They had snuck off with a handful of Dusty's prized Cuban cigars and a twelve-pack of beer that they'd swiped from behind Shelly's bar.

Unfortunately for them, the place they'd chosen for their smoking experiment was the same one where Dusty Muleman had stored several surplus boxes of fireworks. Being the leader in all things stupid, it was Jasper Jr who lit the first cigar, inhaled deeply, gagged violently, and spat the thing twenty feet across the room . . . where it landed in an open crate of bottle rockets, which soon began to ignite, one after the other.

Before long, flames were shooting all over the place. The two party boys were lucky to get out alive.

Jasper Jr was coughing so hard from the cigar that he was useless, so Bull threw him over his shoulder and ran through the smoke and sparks toward an open deck. They landed in the water at the same instant the *Coral Queen*'s fuel tank blew up.

When questioned a few days later, Jasper Jr and Bull denied knowing how the fire started. However, arson investigators couldn't help but notice that both kids had scorched eyebrows and singed earlobes. Jasper Jr wasted no time blaming the boat disaster on his best buddy, the guy who'd saved his life. At that point Bull wisely terminated the friendship and offered a detailed statement to the fire department.

The fact that his own son had burned down the *Coral Queen* was not the worst news that Dusty Muleman would receive. The worst news was that the crime-scene technicians had found something unusual in the charred rubble of the casino boat – a fireproof, waterproof lockbox that was packed with cash.

'More than one hundred thousand dollars,' according to Miles Umlatt's article in the *Island Examiner*, 'all of it in fifty- and one-hundred-dollar denominations.'

Dad's theory was that Dusty had been skimming from the profits of the gambling operation, a crime of great interest to the Internal Revenue Service – and also to the Miccosukee Indians who were supposed to be Dusty's partners.

Fed up with all the rotten publicity, the Miccosukees announced that they intended to sue Dusty for embezzlement, and evict what was left of the *Coral Queen* from their 'tribal grounds', meaning the marina. Dusty's casino scam was scuttled for good.

'What goes around comes around,' Mom remarked after seeing the headlines.

Abbey and I are finally starting to believe it.

A tropical wave blew through the Keys on the Saturday before Labour Day. We were all hanging around the house, waiting for the rain to quit, when the mail arrived.

Mixed in with the usual heap of bills and catalogues was a funny postcard. The picture side showed a scarlet macaw posed on a mossy branch in a beautiful rain forest. The bird was winking and holding an ancient gold coin in its great curved beak.

The message was addressed in a scraggly thin scrawl to 'The Unbelievable Underwoods'.

Dear Paine, Donna, and my two favourite champs,

This is the first postcard I ever wrote, so you should feel honoured. I'm attaching 29,000 pesos in stamps, just to make sure it gets all the way to Florida. If it doesn't, you can blame the shrimper who was supposed to mail it for me when he got to port.

Obviously I'm still alive, which is always sunny news from my point of view. Even better, I've got a red-hot lead on the whereabouts of Amanda

Rose. *With a touch of luck, she and I may be homeward bound by the time you receive this card. On the other hand, I could also be dead, which would seriously mess up my retirement plans.*
But don't bet against the family karma!
Love to all, esp. Abbey and Noah

It was signed, 'Pop'.

We passed the postcard around, then Abbey took it to her bedroom and taped it to the mirror. She put on her emerald earrings and announced that she wasn't taking them off ever again, even for school. Later that afternoon the sky cleared, the wind died, and the seas slicked off.

'How about it?' I asked my father.

'Yeah, let's go,' he said.

We launched at a motel ramp on the ocean side of the island. Mom, Abbey, and I pushed together to slide the bonefish skiff off the trailer, since Dad's hands were still tender from the fractured bones. The casts had been removed a week earlier, but the doctor had warned him to take it easy. You could see he was in pain.

After loading the cooler and fishing rods, we piled in and headed offshore. The little boat was cramped with all four of us on board, but it was fun having Mom there.

The ocean was like a mirror, which made it hard to see the bottom, even with polarized sunglasses. Dad used a GPS to locate the spot, which we had all to ourselves. In less than two hours we caught three dozen snappers. Most of them were small, but we kept four decent ones for dinner.

'What should we name this place?' Abbey asked.

'How about "Dusty's Hole"?' I suggested.

Mom and Dad laughed in approval.

'That's excellent!' Abbey agreed.

I peered over the side of the skiff and squinted against the afternoon glare. I could make out a dark fractured outline on the bottom, the blackened hulk in three large sections.

It was none other than the *Coral Queen*, dearly departed.

A salvage boat was supposed to have hauled it up to the Miami River and loaded it on a garbage barge. Barely three miles into the journey the wreck had broken up during a thunder squall and gone down in twenty-two feet of water. Already herds of hungry fish had made it their new favourite restaurant.

Dusty's Hole.

'It's poetry,' Dad said.

'More like poetic justice,' said Mom.

The morning weather report had spooked everybody else off the ocean and, except for the lighthouse, the horizon remained empty and endless. There wasn't another boat in sight. I lifted Grandpa Bobby's coin from my chest and turned it back and forth in my fingers, the gold catching the sunlight.

'Where would he be coming from? Which direction?' I asked my father.

'Your grandpa? Probably from the southwest.' He made a sweeping gesture. 'Out that way, somewhere.'

'How long will it take him to get here?' Abbey said.

'All depends,' Dad answered quietly.

Mom said, 'Hey, I've got an idea, but we'll need to hurry.'

It was a good idea, too.

We reeled in our lines and stowed the rods. I pulled up the anchor while Dad started the engine, and Abbey dug the camera out of her backpack.

The sky was already turning rosy as we raced toward the west side of the islands, where we'd have the best view. Mom's sunglasses blew off under the Indian Key Bridge, but she told Dad to keep going. We didn't have much time.

The bay was even smoother than the ocean – it looked like pale blue silk. We stopped at Bowlegs Cut, drifting out through the markers on a hard falling tide. Frigate birds soared overhead, and a pod of dolphins rolled past us, herding mullet.

In the distance, somewhere beyond the Gulf of Mexico, the sun was dropping through a coppery and cloudless heaven. None of us dared to say a word, everything seemed so crystal-still and perfect.

Dad edged closer to Mom, and she leaned against his shoulder. Abbey was kneeling in the bow, aiming her camera as the last molten slice of light dripped out of sight.

I sat there dangling my feet in the ripples, watching the day fade away. I was hoping that wherever he might be, Grandpa Bobby was enjoying the same sunset.

When the flash of green came, it lasted for only a magical flick of time – so brief and brilliant and beautiful, I was afraid I'd imagined it.

But then I heard my father say, 'How amazing was *that*?'

So excited, he sounded just like a kid.

CARL HIAASEN has been writing about Florida since his father gave him a typewriter at age six. Then it was hunt-and-peck stories about neighbourhood kickball and softball games, given away to his friends. Now Hiaasen writes a column for the *Miami Herald* and is the author of many bestselling novels, including *Basket Case* and *Skinny Dip*.

Hoot, Hiaasen's first novel for young readers, was the recipient of numerous awards, including the prestigious Newbery Honor.

You can read more about Hiaasen's work at www.carlhiaasen.com.